THIA FINN

Ryder Steel
Thia Finn

ALL RIGHTS RESERVED. This book contains material protected under the International and Federal Copyright Laws and Treaties. **Any unauthorized reprint or use of this material is prohibited.** No part of this book may be reproduced or transmitted in any form or by any means, electronic or mechanical, including photocopying, recording, or by any information storage and retrieval system without express written permission from the author/publisher.

FILE SHARING: Please note that this book is protected under the Digital Millennium Copyright Act (DMCA). It has been made available for your personal use and enjoyment. **No permission has been granted to upload this book onto ANY file-sharing websites.** Doing so is a violation of federal laws and measures have been taken within this file to track the originator of such shared files, should it be found on piracy sites. Thank you for respecting the hard work of the author to produce this content.

WARNING: This is a work of fiction. Names, characters, businesses, places, events and incidents are either the products of the author's imagination or used in a fictitious manner. Any resemblance to actual persons, living or dead, or actual events is purely coincidental.

Disclaimer: The material in this book contains graphic language and sexual content and is intended for mature audiences, ages 18 and older.

ISBN 13: 978-09992358

Edited by Swish Design & Editing
Proofreading by Swish Design & Editing
Book designed and formatted by Swish Design & Editing
Cover design by Jason's Photography
Cover photo model: Wander Aguiar
Cover photographer: Wander Aguiar Photography
Cover image Copyright 2018

Copyright © 2018 Thia Finn
All rights reserved.

A Note For The Reader

If you have not read *Assure Her*, you need to do so before reading *Ryder Steel*. While this book is not a sequel, it is a companion to the original story and requires you to know the sequence of events leading to Ryder's story. Hope you enjoy this final story.

Thia Finn

Dedication

To Lacy Griffin Hendricks and Teale Griffin.
You both are everything I dreamed you would be. My pride in you knows no bounds.

APPROXIMATELY TWENTY-TWO YEARS EARLIER

RYDER

The raspy sound coming out of me happened every time I played in a smoky bar. My lungs gasped for filtered oxygen. It's part of the price musicians pay to make it in this fucking industry. Since none of us had seen twenty-one yet, chilling after our set here seemed like a dumbass idea.

We did it to hang with our growing fan base and network with anyone who listened and might work to promote the band. I made it seem like a chore when the truth was, we loved talking to the people. They fed our need and helped us continue this slow climb. None of us had developed egos like a mega-band might have. For now, we loved hearing from our listeners. We loved knowing they supported us by showing up and buying our music.

Tonight was different, though.

Tonight, I sat at the scarred wooden bar alone.

Tonight, I lingered while the other band members did the dance for us.

Tonight, I tried to wrap my head around what happened a year ago today.

I wasn't one to celebrate anniversaries. Hell, I couldn't tell you the month my parents got married much less the date, but this date holds a fold in my memory.

Today's date was different.

Today's date will always stick with me.

One year ago today marked the last time my eyes took in Laina's gorgeous face, kissed her perfect lips, or heard her lilting voice. She disappeared one year ago today. She walked out of my life with the biggest question hanging over our heads we'll ever need an answer to.

Were we going to be parents? Was a baby in the plan? Were we ready to take on such a huge responsibility as teens straight out of high school? Dammit, if only she were here now to explain where she disappeared to and why.

"Fuck." I lay my head down on my folded arms. "I need a beer."

"I think I can make that happen."

An unfamiliar female voice caused me to raise my head. "Oh, sorry. I was talking to myself."

"Yeah, I do that too, sometimes. Just stop when you start answering your own questions. Makes you look psycho." I stared at the smoking-hot blonde's perfect white smile. Catching the attention of the bartender, she called out, "Two Coors Lights, please."

"Hell, they won't serve me. They already know I'm not old enough to drink. They only hire us to entertain the customers." What a bitch move that was, especially today.

"They'll serve me, and who says I'm not one for double fisting my beer?" Her face lit up again. "Let it sit between us like I'm lining them up. It'll be fine. The bartender's a friend of mine anyway. Honestly, they should let you guys drink if they let you perform."

"That's the truth, but the TABC doesn't see it that way. Those fuckers get hard issuing tickets and pulling permits." Cardboard coasters landed on the bar top before the brunette behind it set the bottles down. My mind said grab it, but not wanting to show my intent, I let the cold glass sit while the two females exchanged looks.

"Thanks, girl. I owe you." The blonde gave the bartender a wink.

"Just don't let his dumbass get drunk."

A bewildered noise left my lips before I could stop it. "Yeah, right. On one damn beer? Doubtful." Sheesh, she knew it wasn't my first.

Her charcoal eyes glanced over the bar top and shook her head before making her way down to the other customers waving Benjamins in her direction.

The frosty bottle called my name, so I snagged it up and looked at the buyer. "Thank you." I tipped the bottle to hers and clinked. "Salud." I took a healthy guzzle instead of sucking down the contents like I wanted to do. By nineteen, I'd chugged my share of beer—one bottle was a sip.

"So, Mr. Musician, I enjoyed the band's show. How long have you guys been playing together?"

"Seems like fucking forever. We're playing here in Austin for our local fans for the next few nights. Been on tour most of this year opening for some big names, but we like to keep our Austin people happy. Hell, we owe them. They gave us our start."

"Forever's a long time."

"Sure as hell is." I looked at her and briefly raised the ends of my lips. I knew this woman's beauty captured attention wherever she went. Her look said older than me but not a cougar by any means. The long legs in the skin-tight black jeans looked damn good. The flesh peeking through the rips teased me. Her spike-heeled short boots made her legs go on forever. Just right for fitting perfectly around my waist while I took her hard and fast against a wall backstage.

Shit, who was I kidding? The last thing I wanted to think about was fucking another woman tonight. I didn't deserve another woman when the only one I wanted was God knows where.

Wrapping both hands around the bottle, I hung my head. I needed to get the fuck out of here and go home to wallow. Why should everyone else be miserable because I was? Yet, here I sat, with a gorgeous woman buying me a drink, pining away for someone I'd never have again.

"So, you've been on tour. Who'd you tour with? Anyone I'd recognize?"

I looked at her wondering what she listened to trying to decide if she would possibly know any of the bands. "We started out playing in dives all over, anywhere we could book a gig. Then we got noticed when we played some dump in Nashville and were invited to be the opening act for No Need."

"Oh, I've heard of them. They've played here in Austin before. I saw them at Antone's. Great show." She held the bottle with three fingers and poked out her pinkie like she drank from a fucking teacup. Watching her tip the bottle that way caused me give a little laugh.

"What?" She put the bottle down. "Are you laughing at me?"

"Uh… hell no. Why would I laugh at you? You bought me a beer. You gave me a reason to smile on a shit night. You're beautiful. What reason would I have to laugh?" Damn, I'm good at covering up for my douchiness.

Her hard stare cut right through me. "Well, I don't know about all that, but I could've sworn I heard you laugh." Her eyes continued to study me. "You know you look a lot better smiling than when you're sulking."

"Sulking, huh?" She had it all wrong.

She took another drink, little finger out. "Uh-huh. What's got you looking like you lost your best friend? From where I'm sitting, seems as though you're living the musician's dream." She glanced back at the stage. "You got yourself a good band, and you're coming off a

Ryder Steel

successful tour. It sounds like you're doing all right to me."

I looked back over my shoulder and watched the rest of the band making their rounds in the audience, shaking hands and signing a few large racks here and there. "Yeah, I guess you're right. I should be grateful."

"Obviously, something's still not right for you tonight."

I emptied the beer and slid the bottle over to the far edge in front of her. "Nope, it's still not right. Guess you could say I lost my best friend, a year ago today."

I rolled around on the stool and put my elbows on the bar top. I needed to leave before I became the quintessential fuck crying in my beer at a bar. "Hey, I'm going to take off. Thanks for the beer. We're playing again tomorrow night at Stubbs. I'll leave you a ticket at Will Call if you want to come hear us play again."

She tipped her bottle in my direction. "I just might do that. Hadn't been down there in a while to listen to a band."

Before I could say anything else, she moved back to face the bar. Guess that was my cue to leave. I knew she'd never show up, but I'd leave a ticket just in case I got it wrong.

RYDER

The soft bed where the band made plans to hang called my name. Finding sleep sounded ludicrous to my addled brain. I needed more than one beer if I was going to pass out. Maybe I should have tried harder with the blonde and brought her home with me. She could fuck my brains out, and then I could drift off mindlessly.

I pulled out my phone and opened the pictures. Laina smiled at me as though life was perfect. She'd taken the selfie of the two of us, her leaning back into me with my arms around her. Dammit, we were so happy sitting beside the cold river water at Zilker Park.

Ryder Steel

I swiped to the next shot. It was us on the university's campus. She loved going there to walk around campus or sit under one of the huge live oaks gracing the lawns between buildings. It made her feel like she belonged. If things hadn't gone south as they did, she'd be there now going to class, meeting up with study groups, and standing in the stadium watching football on Saturdays.

Instead, she vanished. Her parents refused to give up where she went. Before I could find out anything, they disappeared too. Moved to God knows where. Left me high and dry. Even though I thought the whole story seemed strange, the police informed me adults didn't have to get my approval to move away. The men in blue had a good laugh at my expense when I begged them to find Laina's family. After telling me how asinine my request was, they showed me out the door of the station.

So, it's another night. Alone. Depressed. Needy. Wondering about life and why I exist.

Hearing the door bang back against the wall, I rolled over to see who might want to interrupt my pity party.

"Dude. Get the fuck up. We got something to do." Jason rummaged through his bag on the floor at the foot of the bed.

"I'm doing it."

"No way. Get your sorry ass up. Pity Party for one is now over. Repeat, Pity Party for one is now over," he announced it as though through a loudspeaker. "You're too young to be checking out of the world this soon."

He picked up the edge of the mattress, and I found myself hitting the floor with him laughing. "Told you to get up, Ryder Steel. We need your street cred to get us in the club down the street."

"I'm not going to some fucking club."

"Sure as hell are, dude. You need to get out, and we need to get in." He laughed. "Hey, that's a good line for a song. Write that down somewhere." He rummaged around the room looking for something.

"Shut the fuck up and leave me alone." I leaned against the side of the bed as two more bodies walked into the room.

"Shit, he's hibernating again? Ryder, get the fuck up, and let's go." I could only grunt and remember how hard it was for us to get Joel moving in the mornings when we had to drive hours to the next stop.

"Can't y'all just go find someone to occupy your night on your own? I'm tired."

"No, you're not tired, asshat. You're depressed. You know they make meds for that shit, right? Maybe we need to call ol' Mom and Dad and have an intervention for your sorry ass."

I sat up straighter. "Hell no. That's the last thing I want is to make my parents worry about me."

"Then get. The fuck. Up. Which is what I said when I walked in here. Now. Let's go, dude." Joel pulled me up to standing.

"Fine, dammit." I stepped into my boots and pulled out my keys.

The steady thump of club music sounded like shit from the outside when we pulled up around midnight. Every weekend, the line at this place filled in quickly after ten. We hadn't been here in a long time, but I knew the bouncer, and he kept up with our music. The big guy started smiling when I handed off my truck keys to the valet.

"Well, well. I hear there's a new band name now. Steel, right?" He grabbed my hand and wrapped me in his big arm for a hug.

I looked up at him closely. "Yeah, our PR guys with the label wanted something different, so we went with it. Me, Ryder Steel. Sounds badass, huh?"

"Hell yeah, it does." He looked at the four guys behind me. "I'm guessing this is the rest of the band?"

"Yeah, a bunch of dickheads most of the time but damn good musicians." I laughed at the three looking at me. "Well, that's a questionable term on our drummer."

Brett double flipped me off before calling my name. "Ryder Steel." He air-quoted my new name. "You know I'm the best drummer around." He stuck his hand out to meet the big guy. "Brett Cotter."

The third member, our bass player, stepped up from talking to one of the girls who called him over. "Hey, man, I'm Daniel Reyes. Great to meet you." The two shook hands. He was followed by the rhythm guitar player. "Joel Kelley, and this is Jason Glass, our keyboard player."

"Welcome." He pulled back after shaking hands with them and took us all in at once.

The crowd of beautiful women did too. We hadn't grown immune to fans throwing attention our way. We'd played second fiddle with the groupies around the big bands during the tour. It seemed like we always got their leftovers. Sloppy seconds weren't my

Ryder Steel

style for the most part. I hadn't been able to get past the grief I felt over losing Laina. My head wanted to process it as though I'd been through a divorce or worse, her death.

"Come on through, guys. Enjoy. I'll call a cab for you later." Green slipped between our hands as we passed by with a head tip. Always good to acknowledge personal service. A lesson I learned a long time ago— keep the bouncers happy. Never know what might happen that'll require their help.

The roar of the club music filled my ears, and the loud bass vibrated my entire body. Dancers were on the crowded floor doing something the blonde chick with the pointed-tits costume sang about. They kept making hand gestures around their faces. What was up with that shit?

The cacophony of scents filled my nose causing my head to turn in different directions to capture who held each one. Vanilla, fruity, honey, sickeningly sweet, musky, and even sex overwhelmed my nose while walking through to the main bar.

More than once, one of us found a random hand touching us indiscriminately. Being last, I had the pleasure of having each ass cheek rubbed, pinched, and even a slight swat. Who said women were the only ones who felt violated in clubs?

P a g e | **13**

Thia Finn

I drew the line on having some random woman grab my dick, though. I managed to stop that action each time before contact was made. I'd simply push the hand back and offer a slight smile to the owner, which thankfully tonight was only female. It wasn't always that way. Guess you can't blame a guy for trying, but I prefer a soft female against my skin.

RYDER

It only took a few drinks before I needed to get the hell out of there. The loud sounds did nothing to keep the demons from firing around in my head. Something more pressed on me tonight, but I couldn't pin it down. The vibrations from my phone sent unpleasant feelings down my leg each time a call or message came through, but I managed to ignore them. The last thing I wanted to do was try to talk to someone tonight.

The Jack and Coke slid back and forth in the short span between my hands on the tabletop. After the first two, the third did nothing for me telling me it was time to blast off.

Thia Finn

"Dude," Daniel started in on me. "You going to get out of your head for even a few minutes tonight? The look on your face even scares me, much less all the hot girls who've been sniffing around the table."

"Good. Don't need a woman. I've got the best woman."

Jason put his arm around my shoulders. "No, Ryder, you don't. Laina's gone. We've been over this for a full fucking year. She's no longer your Laina, no longer your woman."

"Fuck off." I moved out of his hold. "She'll always be the woman I want."

"No, dude. She won't." This time it was Daniel.

"All of you fuck off." *Who were they to tell me this?*

My phone kept going and going this time. I finally pulled it out to see I'd missed a shit ton of calls from my parents' number. "What the hell. Something's wrong." Every one of my family had reached out.

"What's going on?" Daniel stepped up behind me. I'd known Daniel all my life. We'd been friends since the first day of kindergarten. He was new to Smithville and stood alone, so I threw the kickball at him on the playground. He grabbed it up joining my friends like we'd known each other all five years of our lives. Now, fifteen years later, we were still

P a g e | 16

throwing things at each other, even a few fists on occasion.

He saw all the calls he knew to be my family since we'd practically lived at one house or the other for all those years.

"Man, you better call home." The look he wore mimicked mine.

I nodded and headed for the exit door, him fast on my heels.

I hated even to hear the phone ring on the other end, the smell of urine burned my nose as I waited in the back alley.

"Oh, Brax."

"What's wrong, Mom? Is it Dad?" I sucked in a big breath afraid of her answer.

"No, honey. It's not your dad. Here, talk to him." The strained voice told me she tried to hold back tears, but when Dad said hello to me, her distinct sobs echoed in the background.

"Dad, what's going on? Just tell me." Yelling into the phone gained his attention.

"Son, we got word a few minutes ago about Laina."

"What? What kind of word? Where is she? Who did you hear it from?" The questions flew even though I knew he didn't have time to answer between each one.

"Calm down, Brax." He paused. "You see, son, her aunt called. Said she knew you'd want to know."

"Know what, Dad?"

"Laina's dead, son. She was killed in a car accident. She's been living with her aunt all this time in Washington, D.C."

"I... I..." No words formed. I backed against the wall and slid down dropping my phone on the concrete.

Daniel picked it up examining the flipped-open screen.

He spoke into the phone. "Hey, Mr. Whitmore, it's Daniel. What's happening?" He held the phone between us so we could both hear.

"I know this is hard, and we don't know much. The aunt only said that Laina had talked about you the entire time she lived there, so she felt like you should know what happened. Laina's car was t-boned at a red light, and she was killed instantly. The woman didn't say if she was alone or not. She didn't say anything about a baby either. Your mom point blank asked. All she said was Laina was alone in the car."

I screamed at the phone, "Did the lady leave a number I can call?" I jerked it away from Brett.

"No, it was a house phone, Brax. We've already tried to dial it back."

"Shit. This isn't right, Dad. It's not right. I've already lost her once. I never got to tell her goodbye. Never, Dad. Never." I couldn't stop the tears or the wailing. "It's not fair. Why, Dad? What did I do so wrong? You know all I ever did was love her, Dad. I love her so much still. Why, Dad?"

"Listen, Brax. Son, you didn't do anything wrong. We all know how much you two loved each other. All of this was out of your hands. They took it all away. They had all the power here."

"But I need her in my life, Dad. I need her. I've waited a whole year. A year today, Dad."

"I know, Brax. I'm so sorry, son." He took a deep breath. "Braxton, why don't you let us come up to Austin and pick you up?"

"When's the funeral, Dad? I need to go to the funeral." I began pacing. I could get to D.C. on a flight tonight. I could be there to say goodbye to her one last time. I know she'd hear me when I got to see her beautiful face one last time.

There was no sound on the other end. "Dad?"

"The funeral's already happened."

"No way, Dad? When? Where is she?" I yelled at him for no reason, but I couldn't keep the anger from my voice. This couldn't be happening. Not again. No fucking way this scene was playing through my head

Thia Finn

again. There was no repeat button in my brain, so why did it feel like it?

"She's buried here in Smithville, Brax. They had a private service. No one knew. I'm sorry. Apparently, they had the body shipped in a few days ago and had a graveside service without notifying anyone. That's all the lady would tell us. I'm so sorry they did this to you, son. I don't know what to say."

"Nooo." My brain was ready to explode. "Nooo."

Chapter 4

ONE YEAR LATER

RYDER

"Goodnight L.A. Thanks for having us!" The noise level made my closing barely audible even through the speakers.

The band made their way off stage to the thunderous roar of crowd noises. After two encores, we were done. With adrenaline flying, we opened the door to the green room that now held all our own stipulations.

In the last two years, the band had exploded into the music scene in nuclear fashion. Steel flew high as a whole, but none higher than me. I wrote the entire first album in less than two months after learning of

Laina's death. Darkness and misery poured out of each stroke of the pencil and every chord I strummed.

The bus rolled down the highway from show to show, and lyrics tumbled from my mind, or maybe my heart, onto the pages of my notebook. I couldn't be bothered with using a computer like some musicians were moving toward. I needed paper and pencil to make my music happen. Nothing more.

Daniel came up behind me as I watched the groupies gearing up to take on whatever the guys were into tonight.

"You hanging around tonight for some fun and games?" He nodded in Jason's direction where a panty-less woman's skirt hiked up around her waist as she ground down on him.

"No, man. You know that's not happening. I got some songs to lay down, though. I'll see y'all at the bus later. Enjoy some pussy for me." I grinned at him, picked up a bottle of Jack, and walked to the doorway.

I called over the room. "Y'all be good children and don't miss the fucking bus."

"I got your fucking bus right here, Ryder Steel." Brett grabbed his junk over his jeans and shook. "Hang around, Ryder. Someone will feel sorry for you, and you might get lucky." Everyone laughed, and I gave a half-smile at his attempted humor. They knew I

Ryder Steel

wouldn't stay to watch the debauchery. I'd never be a part of it, either.

Security for tonight flanked me back to the bus. Our home on wheels' door opened, and they watched me walk up to the top of the steps. I turned back and saw Todd give me a sharp nod. He knew what I wanted, or in this case, needed for tonight. He always took care of me.

The steady decline in constantly being high or wanting to be high kept me moving forward. I didn't know if I wanted to keep going most nights. What I wanted was to tempt fate at every turn.

The top to my handle of Jack hit the floor as I took a drink directly from the bottle. The fire sliding down my throat woke up my senses. The thirst I knew was coming needed to be slaked ahead of the hit.

I pulled out the tubing, tied it off, and prepped the needle waiting for me. After another healthy pull on the bottle, I stared at the white horse calling me to take a ride. The sudden rush I was about to have would pull me under and let my brain rest. That's what I thought it did.

The vein popped up after a couple of taps, and I eased in the needle. As I pressed the plunger, I heard the door open to the bus.

P a g e | **23**

"Fuck," I growled as I pushed harder. "Who's out there?"

"Dude. What are you doing back there?" Daniel yelled from the front steps followed by some giggles. "I needed to come pick up my keys. We're going for a ride."

While he spoke, I eased down on my bed. *Damn, it felt so fucking good. The warmth spread over me, taking me under. Taking me to a location where I felt best—floating.*

I heard the door slide back.

"What the fuck, Ryder? What have you done?"

"Get out." I thought I yelled. "Get the fuck out now."

"No, dude."

"Yeah, I'm fine. It's all going to be good now."

"Like hell, it will."

I heard him talking to someone, maybe on his phone. I didn't know or care. I felt good. I felt free. I could make it through another night, alone. I could live for another day, alone.

Ties held me down when I woke up. "Help," I tried to scream. "Help me."

The metal door swung open to a big guy in scrubs.

"Good morning, Mr. Steel."

"Where the fuck am I?" The Mojave Desert lived in my mouth. The words barely escaped in more than a whisper. Looking around, I recognized nothing. This couldn't be good.

"You're in Arizona."

"How the hell did I get here? I was in Los Angeles yesterday."

"Actually, that was three days ago. They brought you here three days ago." The blue-clad giant started at my ankles untying the binds.

"Who did this to me?" Someone had to get me here, and I knew my band wouldn't do it. They loved me. I was Ryder fucking Steel. I owned this band.

"I'm not sure about that, Mr. Steel."

I watched as he loosened the straps on my wrist. "Thanks, man. It's Ryder." I rolled my stiff wrist around when he finished.

"No problem." He completed his task and sat on the rolling stool by the bed. "You want to try to stand up? Maybe take a leak on your own?"

Thia Finn

I glanced back at him wondering how I'd been doing before now. "I guess. Yeah. I gotta piss like a racehorse now that you've mentioned it."

"Okay, let's do it." He unfolded his long body and stood beside the bed. "Let's start with your feet on the floor and see how far you get."

I thought I had this and tried to throw my legs over. Yeah, they barely moved. My head jerked back up looking at him. "What's going on?"

"Dude, you haven't moved on your own in three days. You can't expect everything to go back to working like before so quickly. Let's do this together."

He pulled my legs over to the side, and I slid forward to the edge of the bed. When my feet hit the white tiled floor, I winced at the cold.

"Yeah, everything's going to seem sensitive for a while. It'll get better. Now, I want you to stand and hold on to me."

I eased off the bedside, my legs wobbling. "Guess I'm more unsteady than I thought."

He nodded. "Just stand but don't try to walk yet."

I stood holding onto his forearms and looked at him. "How the fuck did this happen?"

"Apparently, the dosage you took was too much for your body. You OD'd on H. Do you remember taking it?"

P a g e | 26

"No, I don't remember shit at this point." Standing made me sweat.

"Good thing one of your band members found you when he did. You'd just injected the substance. He saved your life."

"Why?" I looked at this man who held me up.

"Why?" he asked back. "Why what?"

"Why did he save me?"

"Hmm… that's a question you'll have to ask him. Don't you think we all need saving at some point?"

I didn't answer.

"Okay, you seem more stable. Try a few steps and see what you got."

The two of us managed to get me into the pristine white bathroom where I leaned on the wall long enough to piss.

Exhaustion set in by the time I made it back to bed. All I wanted to do was sleep.

"Mr. Steel?"

Sunshine beamed across my face. I held out my hand to block the rays. "What? Can someone shut the damn blinds? That's too fucking bright."

"Sure thing." I heard movement, and the room darkened slightly. "You're going to get up today, Mr. Steel. Doctor's orders."

"Fuck the doctor. I'm fine right here."

"No, sir. You're not. Come on."

"I don't want to get out of this fucking bed. Now leave me the hell alone." My feeble attempt at swatting the hand away only caused me to almost fall out of the bed.

"Let's do this together, Mr. Steel."

"No."

"Sorry, I can't take no for an answer."

"Like hell, you can't. I feel sure I'm paying to stay here, so I'm the boss."

"Yes, you are paying dearly. But while you're in this room, and I'm on duty, I'm the boss. I say you're getting out of this bed today. You need a bath and food."

"Fuck that. I couldn't eat if I tried."

"We'll start slow. Liquids."

"I could use some liquids. How about a fifth of my old buddy Jack?"

"Uh... that's a big no. How about a bottle of apple juice or a Gatorade? We have all flavors."

"Sounds like shit."

"No, we don't have shit flavor, but the other clients think the purple's pretty good."

"How about some water, then?"

The crisp sound of water pouring over ice broke the silence. The man handed me a tall glass with a straw. After a few sips, I handed it back.

"Okay. Now you're getting up."

"Fuck. Are you going to do this to me every day?"

"Yes, either someone else or me so you might as well get it in your head, you're getting up from now on."

This same routine went on for what seemed like months. In reality, it might have been a few days. My brain didn't want to process any of it.

"Good morning, Ryder."

"What's good about this shit? I fucking need to get out of here." I rolled over facing the wall. "Who says I have to stay? I can check out anytime I want, right?"

"Let's have you talk to Dr. Grimes first. See what he thinks about that idea."

"Then get his sorry ass in here. I'm ready to leave."

The door closed behind my daily visitor. This couldn't be my life. Not much time passed before I heard the door open again.

"Mr. Steel? I'm Dr. Grimes. You wanted to have a visit?"

"Hell no. I don't want to have a visit. I want to leave."

"You agreed to stay for thirty days when you came in."

"No way did I commit myself to thirty days of this shit."

"Actually, we have the papers saying you did. Care to sit up and talk to me in my office?"

"Will it get me out of here sooner?"

"Possibly."

"Then let's do this." I rolled over and put my feet on the floor. I could do it this time.

"Let's walk to my office." He put his hand out to show the way from my door.

From the looks around this place, I knew I was paying top dollar to be here. Everything about it spoke money and luxury. I didn't give a fuck, though. I wanted out. I needed out. People depended on me for

Ryder Steel

their livelihood. The band depended on me. It was time to get back to what I did best.

Dr. Grimes sat down in a chair in front of a sleek desk and held out a hand suggesting I join him in the mirror-imaged seating.

"So, Ryder Steel. It's a pleasure to meet you."

I looked at this guy out of one eye. Whose pleasure were we talking about? Couldn't be mine. I was miserable. My head hurt. My eyes hurt. Fuck, I hurt in general.

"Why am I here, doctor?"

"Ryder. May I call you that?" I nodded. "You're here because you overdosed on heroin. You were found quickly by one of your bandmates, and the doctors were able to revive you."

"Great." My enthusiasm lacked.

"Is it? Do you remember anything about the drugs you injected?"

I thought about what he asked. "Not really. Were they something special?"

"In a broad sense, no, but in your case, it was too much."

I nodded my head.

"The real question is, was the amount you used intentional?"

Thia Finn

"Are you asking if I was trying to kill myself with it? If that's what you want to know, the answer is no and yes."

"I'm not sure it can be both."

"Sure it can. If I died, it'd be all right. If I lived, that's okay, too."

"Your friends and family would disagree with you. They've been extremely worried about you since you arrived."

"Oh yeah. Could have fooled me. I haven't seen any of those fuckers show up here."

The doctor leaned forward and retrieved a paper on his desk. "That doesn't mean they haven't been here. You can't have visitors yet." He turned the paper around, and signatures I recognized covered the form.

I took it from him. "These people have all been here?"

"Yes, or they called. They all tried to come the first day, but we informed them it would be a while before you can work up to having visitors."

"Well, shit. I want to see my friends, explain to them—"

"And that time will come." He looked at me over the top of his old-man half-glasses.

We spent the next hour talking about basically nothing. He asked ridiculous questions he should already have the answers to, and I tried not to look at him like he was a moron.

"Okay, I think I've grilled you enough for one day. Do you have any questions for me?"

"Yes." I looked up at him. "Why the hell do good people die?"

He folded back his notebook to the beginning. It was plain, white, and sterile. He finally looked up at me and gave me a hint of a smile. "That's a good question, Ryder. I wish I had the answer to it. Not everything in our lives is in our control, and your question is a perfect example of it."

I stood and walked out the door. Obviously, he didn't know any more than I did.

The next few days all passed the same. Someone showed up to make me get up. Dr. Grimes tried to get me to tell all. I had nothing to say because I knew he didn't have the answers. I had to give it to the guy for trying, though. He never seemed exhausted over my repetitive nothingness.

On Saturday morning, I immediately knew something different was going on. Same guy, different day, showed up, but this time, he had clothes in his hands instead of my usual white wardrobe.

"Morning. Here's some of your own clothes to wear today." He handed the stack to me.

Thia Finn

"Oh, really? Why do I need these unless I'm leaving?" I eyed him while still laying on my pillow.

"Dr. Grimes is going to let you have some visitors today." He smiled at me like he knew this would make me happy.

"Hell yeah." I sat up. "It's about fucking time. Who's coming? Do I get to choose who I want to see?"

"Whoa, slow down, speed racer. I don't know the answer to any of your questions. I'm only told what I need to know. My job today is to make sure you're ready to see visitors, and from the first actual enthusiasm I've seen out of you since you've arrived, I'm going to say yes, you're ready."

"Dude, I was born ready. I'm so ready to get the hell out of here, I'll take whatever I can get." Scooping up the clothes, I disappeared into the bathroom.

While I showered, I thought about who I truly wanted to see. Now I had a few minutes to think about the fact that anyone I saw would want to ask questions, my overzealous attitude slightly slipped away.

Dressed, I stepped out to where my helper waited. "You want to shave some of that fur off your face?" My unkempt beard stared at me in the mirror. On the road, the label's makeup people made sure it looked perfect every night.

Ryder Steel

"Yeah, the lumberjack look might scare someone. You got a razor for me?" I turned to look at him.

He stood. "Sorry man, you have to leave the door open, so I can watch you with it." He shrugged his shoulders.

"Right. I get it. You're doing your job. We've all got them, unless this is some kind of kink you've got. You know, watching other men shave or something like that." I grinned as I said it.

My true personality reached the surface a little more each day. Using H only happened a few times over the past two years. No drug was my favorite, and the booze I could take or leave. My guy helped me out with what he could score along the way. He'd never let me down before the night of the overdose.

Shit needed to be hashed out with the band and our support people before Steel could be a band again. With no contact on the outside, I had no idea what had been done already, but hopefully, that would be remedied with these visitors.

Chapter 5

RYDER

The apprehensive step into Dr. Grimes' office ramped up my anxiety with not knowing who to expect. The surprise landed on my shoulders because the doctor sat alone behind his desk.

"Good morning, Ryder." He stood and motioned me in. "Come in. Gabriel says you're excited to be wearing street clothes."

"Yeah, it feels good to wear something of my own." I tugged on the hem of the nondescript black t-shirt. "Don't get me wrong. I'm all about lounging around, but I'm done with that." The chair sighed under my weight as I sat opposite him. Leaning back, I draped my arm across the one beside me. With a straight look at his face, the question popped out without any thought. "So, doc, who's coming to see me? Not that it matters. At this point, I'd be happy to see anyone."

He looked at the top of the file before he spoke. "Well, I wanted to talk to you about visitors first. We normally don't allow them this soon in the program. After consulting with your caregivers and staff, we all feel like you'd benefit from some contact with your people."

"Hell yeah, I would. My band is out there fucking off without me. There's a genuine need to know what's going on." The desperation in my voice rang loud, so imagining what the doctor thought scared me.

"The thing is, Ryder, you have no control over anything outside this facility at this point. Your concentration lies with getting yourself together so you can continue with the band."

"What? There's no doubt in my mind I'll be continuing to lead Steel, doctor."

"Yes, I know you believe that, but the temptation to use will be strong. Face it, the availability will be all around you. We both know, along with the band comes the alcohol, drugs, sex, or whatever your cravings may be at the time. It's up to us to help you find a way to control this need. Of course, the easiest way to control yourself is to stay away from it."

"That's not going to happen, doc. Those three vices are a fact of life in the damn business." I took a deep breath and looked back up at him. "You're going to have to show me how the hell to work around it and not be tempted."

He chuckled a little. "Ryder, we can teach you all day long, but unless you possess the desire not to use, it's not going to work. We'll do all we can, but the bottom line at staying clean is all on you. If you want it, you can do it."

All I could do was nod my head because I already knew what he said to be true. The monkey stood directly on my shoulders. "I want it, doctor, but I have some damn problems I need to deal with. Some things I can't get out of my head." Taking another deep breath, "Some things I don't know how to let go."

"And that's where we come in, Ryder. If you want to do this and will let us help you, we can show you how to let them go or at least how to deal with the situation when it starts taking over you again. It's a matter of trust on your part. Do you trust me... us, enough to work with our group?"

Thinking about letting Laina go scared the shit out of me. I never wanted to forget her, but continuing to live this way marked a slow descent into total destruction. The band needed me too much to let that happen. We all had our skeletons but none as bad or as the fucked-up ones that had taken my mind hostage. Damn it, I needed to man up and get on with my life.

I stared directly at him. "You're right, doc. This is all on me. You think you can help me crawl out of this hellhole I'm stuck in?"

He stood and stuck out his hand to shake mine. "Yes, Ryder. We'll help you, and you've finally taken the first step to improvement." We shook on it. "Now, let's talk about visitors."

The guys stood around in the outdoor courtyard where they'd been told to wait. When I turned the corner to head out the door, I stopped and watched them for a second. They were my family. We'd been together for over five years now. Even when we did dumbass stuff, we stuck together. We always had each other's back. Our past told me they wouldn't let me down now either. My need for their help weighed heavily, but I hoped they were willing to raise up and help pull me through one more time.

Joel spotted me through the tall glass window and grinned.

"Okay, Ryder Fucking Steel. You're on. Let's do this," I said out loud to myself.

"Well, look who the cat's dragged up." Joel met me at the doorway and took my hand but pulled me in close patting me on the back. "Dude, you look good, damn good."

Daniel, Brett, and Jason joined in and took their turn greeting me in the same way. I knew counting on these guys would never be an issue. We *were* family.

We sat in the chairs with the morning sun illuminating every direction I looked. For the first time in forever, the five of us stayed in one place and held a real conversation. I knew they kept it light avoiding the burning questions in the beginning. Hell, they might completely skip the important stuff, so I brought it up myself.

"Okay, so now we're all over the bullshit of what's been happening, I need to talk to y'all about what we're trying to tap dance around." Terror crossed their faces. Never realizing how hard my fuck-up was for them, making this right became even clearer to me.

"First off, damn, I'm glad y'all agreed to come see my sorry ass, but it's been better that they wouldn't let you come before now."

"We tried hard, Ryder," Daniel started. "We wanted to know you were okay, but they wouldn't tell us shit."

"I gotta tell y'all the truth. I'm not okay. Better, yes. Okay to leave, no. The doctor thinks if I stay for six more weeks, I can look at leaving with hopes of never returning. I'll probably still see a counselor for a while after I leave." I hung my head hating to admit the truth. "Maybe forever, but I'll be able to leave and resume playing with the band."

They all spoke at once agreeing the news was great. "I'm going to need all of your help, especially in the beginning. This problem I'm having isn't going to go away. Once an addict, always an addict. There's only one good thing about it... I didn't use H but a few times, and never on a regular basis."

Jason focused on me while the others refused to meet my eyes as I looked at each one of them. "Hell, Ryder, we should've been more aware of what was really going on with you. You know, how deep you were in. We fucked up in that department."

Brett joined him. "Yeah, we did fuck it up. Maybe we didn't want to admit how bad it was getting because then we'd have to deal with it. None of us wanted to get up in your shit."

"Right, none of us wanted to face the fact that deep down we knew you were hurting," Joel finally spoke up. "I mean, we weren't down with it, but we all knew you were like legit trying to cope the best you could. It sucked big ones that you got that way, and we should have been baggin' on you to management. Like, you know, we aren't narcs. Besides, we never saw you hanging out with the lowlifes or anything."

We all stared at Joel with blank faces. I finally looked at the other three. "Who is this guy? I mean, like did he totally spend like the last three weeks jetting to the valley to hang with the mall chicks or something?" We all laughed so hard both at Joel and my reply to him.

Brett finally spoke up. "No man, he found one in Austin who had moved from California, and she's managed to Val-speak him into a new generation. Like totally." We all laughed again as Joel turned all shades of red in the face.

"Shut the fuck up. Y'all know what I was saying."

We all chimed in together. "Totally."

Our conversation felt lighter for the rest of the visit. We discussed band business, family, and when I would be getting back to Texas. Since the world knew

Ryder Steel

I was in rehab, the remaining dates of the tour had been canceled. The flipside of fame and notoriety was life in front of a camera, and the world knew your worst secrets.

We made our way to the front door when Daniel spoke up. "I got something for you. We called, and they told us it would be okay to bring it. It's in the rental car. Let me get it."

He sprinted out the entryway, and I turned with a puzzled look at the others. "Are y'all sure it's okay with the doc?"

"Yeah, we called before we got on the jet this morning to double check with him," Brett answered.

I nodded. "Hey, thanks for coming all this way. I appreciate what y'all are doing out there to keep me out of the fucking spotlight."

"Dude. We've been trying to like jet out here, but they totally wouldn't let us," Joel said.

"Dude. I don't know if I can like fucking take you talking like this all the damn time."

"Oh, right. I'll try to break that shit over the next few weeks."

The door opened before we could laugh at him again.

"My guitar!" I almost cried in front of the guys. I took it from Daniel as though he handed me a precious piece of gold. "Thanks, guys. You don't know how much I've missed my girl. They've got a piano in here that I've banged around on, but it's not my guitar. I've written enough lyrics to fill a notebook, but hell, the music plays on a constant record in my head. I'm anxious to get it down on paper.

"Well, that's damn good to hear because we brought you another notebook, too." Daniel pulled the folded spiral from his back pocket. "We figured you'd need it until you're able to leave."

"I'd kiss y'all for this, but then the doctor might think something more was going on and want to keep me longer." We all laughed as I handed the case over to the gatekeeper at the door so it could be checked for anything other than a guitar. I looked back at the guys. "They take fucking security serious at this place." They all nodded as though they understood.

We shook and hugged before they passed through the glass doors. I looked at the receptionist and stepped out holding the door open. We weren't allowed out in front of the facility, but I knew her hawk eyes never left me, so I risked it.

The horn honked, and we waved at each other as they drove off. I turned and pulled the door closed behind me making sure the older woman watched, then walked back to my room with my girl and the new notebook in my hand. Nothing stood between me and songwriting now. I couldn't wait to take it out of the case.

SIX WEEKS LATER

"Yes, Mr. and Mrs. Whitmore, I understand." Dr. Grimes spoke quietly into his phone. "Ryder, I know this isn't what you wanted. No one wants to return to rehab but in this case, it's more of a time for dealing with the memories that tried to keep you down the first time. The loss of your girlfriend presents new problems. The easy thing to do is self-medicate with substances and alcohol, and we both know where that's going to get you."

I leaned back in the chair and stared at the ceiling. "Fuck yeah, I know but it doesn't make it any easier, doctor. I always had hope before. I hoped that Liana would come to her senses and find me. I hoped she'd have my kid and realize I was out there waiting for her. I wanted to play every little town on the map with the hope my face would turn up in a photo and she would know who Ryder Steel was."

I stood and paced the room. "But hell no. None of that happened. And now," I turned and looked him right in the eyes. "Now there's no reason to continue any of this. No reason to make music, to tour, to go home, to do shit. Now, there's no damn reason left for me to live. If I can't have what I want most in life, why bother?"

He leaned forward in his chair and stared right back at me. The look said he meant every word about to spew from his mouth. "And that, Ryder Steel, is the reason you are here."

Chapter 6

PRESENT DAY
TAKEN FROM *ASSURE HER*
DAY OF RECONNECTION - 13 RECORDING STUDIO

CHANDLER

The man I knew as a big rock and roll legend, covered in tats and piercings on every visible surface and a face weathered beyond his years, couldn't speak to me. He fell to his knees in front of me and laid his head on my lap. The tears that flowed freely from him matched the ones I could no longer hold back.

KeeMac and the other band members from Assured Distraction quietly stepped out to give the two of us the privacy we needed to cope with the tragedy causing our twenty plus years of separation.

Fathers and daughters shouldn't be forced to endure a loss like this.

Who had the right to take away a lifetime of childhood memories?

After we both had time to collect ourselves, he regained his composure and spoke. "I was praying you would forgive me, Chandler, for running out on you like I did at our first meeting. I was a coward, plain and simple. I knew it when I saw you," he finally said to me. He looked me straight in the eyes before taking out contacts revealing aqua blue eyes matching my own.

"Oh. My. God!" I couldn't believe what I was seeing. "Why? Why did you cover them up?"

"The first douchebag manager we had said they were too washed out under the stage lights, so I started wearing brown ones. The two colors together made my eyes look wicked, and I was a kid then so looking 'wicked' sounded like a damn good idea. By the time we made it big, everyone was so used to them, I never changed. Only my inner circle and family has ever seen me without them."

He stood up and opened his arms asking for permission. When I nodded he pulled me to him, wrapped me in a bear-hug, and lifted me off the ground. "You don't know what's running through my mind, Chandler. I have so many things I want to ask you, so much I want to know about your entire life. I'm so sorry I wasn't there for you, but I never knew.

"Your grandparents took my precious Laina away from me. We were lovesick kids, Chandler. Please believe they refused to tell me anything about her. Said it was for both our own good. Fucking people. They kept the greatest thing I've ever done from me all this time. I could kill them all!"

"I don't understand how you never found me before, Ryder. Didn't you ever try to look for my mom and me?" So many questions plagued me, but this one I wanted the answer to so badly.

He pulled me back to the couch. "I didn't know about you, Chandler. You don't know what happened to me during that time. The band had been trying so hard to get our name out there and get signed with a label. Hell, all we ever wanted was to play our music and be on top. When we finally got the chance to go, we had to jump at it, but it meant leaving your mom behind. She was getting everything ready to leave for University of Texas the moment classes started in the fall. When this shit started, it all happened so fast." He repeated the story about the night Laina shared with him the possibility of being pregnant.

"We didn't get back to Austin 'til after 3:00 a.m. When I finally rolled my sorry ass into bed, I slept most of the next day. I called your mom as soon as I woke and got nothing. No one would answer the damn phone. I went over there, and the place was locked up tight, both cars gone. I couldn't find them anywhere. I even went to the police, and they took one look at me and informed me they had no fucking reports of any wrongdoings. Told me adults could leave without my permission. Someone disconnected her phone the next day. After that, I heard nothing. My parents tried to help, too. When her parents came home a week later without Laina, the sorry pieces of shit refused to give me any information other than she was doing what she wanted, and it had nothing to do with me. She never tried to contact me, so I figured they were telling the truth. I had no idea where to start looking. Believe me when I say, I would have gone to the ends of the earth trying to find your mom. I loved her, Chandler.

"It was the worst fucking time in my life, Chandler. You have to know that." He captured my hands between his and kissed them. "The band was opening for a huge band, and we were getting noticed by a lot of labels. Our fame kinda blew up. I was totally fucked up, though, after losing your mom. I started drinking more and then came the drugs. Hell, they were easy to come by with so many assholes out there ready to deliver. A year later, I was in rehab for a couple of months." He lowered and shook his head remembering the lost years. "I wrote some of our best music to date while I was in there. That's where *Stolen* came from. It was and still is our biggest hit. The lyrics to that song came out of me during the worst days of my life.

"Shortly after I got out of that damn rehab, my parents received the news that Laina was dead. I went completely off the deep end. I hadn't seen her. I never got to say goodbye. I couldn't handle it all. My first thought was I needed a drink and something to make me forget. Honestly, I wanted to forget it all." Ryder stood and grabbed the back of his chair.

Looking down at me, he said something I knew he wished he didn't have to say. "I was ready to die, darlin'. When I started talking that kind of crazy, the guys took action. Got my parents involved, and they got me back into the rehab facility for the second time." The look in his eyes told me his confession hurt him deeply, but since he felt the need to come clean about the entire situation, hearing it all was necessary.

He turned away and took a deep breath. "Those were really dark days, but I came out a hell of a lot better for it. I truly dealt with my grief and my depression. Ultimately, I dealt with my addictions." He whipped back around to face me, to show he faced his demons head-on. "I fight the fucking addictions every single day. Thank God, I worked through it all, though." Ryder sat down beside me and added, "I still see my therapist occasionally."

I reached for his hands and held them in mine this time. I needed the connection and believed he did, too, considering what he'd told me. Looking at the anguish Ryder was going through told me the kind of man he was.

He said nothing for a second, and I waited for him to regain some composure, before he continued, "I'm so sorry I left you like that when I saw you in Denver. I couldn't deal. The old demons rushed my brain with memories better left forgotten. Leaving you standing there was difficult, but I recognized the signs. I needed help to come to terms with them even after all these years. I've spent the last weekend in the facility for some intense sessions with my doctor.

"When I saw you with my own eyes staring back at me and heard your story, it was like reliving the worst fucking nightmare of my life. Now that I've had time to get my head together, I realize what an idiot I was to walk away. At that moment, it was the best thing I could do for both of us." A line appeared between his drawn brows.

"Please say you'll forgive me?" The sincerity on his face almost gutted me. "I'll understand if you don't or need time to consider everything I've told you. Fuck, I know it's a lot, Chandler. I'm ready to deal with the blowback from my actions, but I hope you'll find a place in your heart to forgive one sorry-ass, shell-shocked Dad," he pleaded with tears in his eyes.

All I could do was wrap him in a hug and hold on for dear life. We found each other, *finally*. And I had no intentions of letting him go. For better or worse, we had a start to being a family. A relationship void of lies and secrets. A place to start building something we could both be a part of. Together, father and daughter.

RYDER

Sitting in the jet going to our next stop on the tour, I watched KeeMac and Chandler tangled together on a long couch. No doubt about it, they were in love. It made my heart happy to see my daughter had found her person. I knew she searched for someone to love her, especially now with her adopted parents gone.

Thia Finn

The kid lived a lie, but the truth almost tore her apart from what they told me.

The idea I had something to do with her pain nearly gutted me every time it crossed my mind. Knowing I had hurt her again after she found me made it even worse, but with the shape I was in, there was no way I would attempt to reconcile with her until I could get my head back on straight. Thank God Dr. Grimes agreed to see me on the spur of the moment. He knew what was happening could cause me to do something I'd later regret.

Here I was, though, flying on our jet, watching my daughter sleep across from me. I smiled to myself knowing life couldn't get much better.

"What are you smiling about?" Joel took notice as he sat in the chair next to me.

"The fact that after all these years, I have a kid, and she accepts me flaws and all."

"We tried to tell you that for a long time. The love you have for a child is unconditional."

"I know. I guess it took her forgiving me before I could forgive myself."

Joel nodded. "This Austin trip rates as one of the best in a long time."

"Hell, it's the absolute best for me."

Ryder Steel

"Maybe now you'll agree to come home more often. Shit, maybe we'll even play for the hometown again. It's been years since we've played in Austin."

"I know, and I regret we didn't. Maybe I'd have found her before now if we had."

"Doubtful, and besides, you can't change the past. No use in letting it bother you any longer."

"You're right. Can't change what's done, but we can make it a helluva future."

"Yeah, who knows, the great Ryder Steel might even let himself find a woman and fall in love."

"The hell you say. Who'd want this old, used up rocker?"

"Dude, you're barely in your forties, not your eighties." Joel laughed.

"I don't know. I feel eighty some days." My fingers raked through the longer hair I still had on the top of my head. I wore it long when we started the band and pulled it up to secure it with a leather string. That mess got old though, with it constantly in my face, so I chopped it off.

"Isn't that the damn truth? I feel it every day when I crawl out of bed. Maybe we should have taken better care of ourselves when we were their age." He nodded over at the sleeping kids.

"You're damn straight we should have, but we still rock better than most of them." We bumped fists before I laid back in my chair and closed my eyes. "I think it's time for my siesta."

"I hear ya." He reclined his chair.

I don't know who snored faster between the two of us.

G'ANNA

"Don't leave until we compare schedules, please." I looked down at my personal assistant and smiled.

"What would I do without you?" I opened the appointment app on my phone. "I have a consult with another band at ten, and then I'm heading over to the studio to see what time I need to leave to catch up with the bands. Steel and Assured Distraction left this morning."

"Right. You plan to hit every U.S. stop with them until they leave for Europe?" Trudy never took her eyes off the screen as she scrolled around the planner.

"Yeah, probably. Only a few shows are playing here before crossing the pond. They must need some warm-up shows or something. It's their first time on tour together. I'll catch up only for the shows, they want new pics taken overseas. I have a couple of other bands to shoot along the way."

"Yeah, and don't forget your cousin's wedding in a few months. She's going to want bridal portraits, the day of pictures." She rolled her hand in the air indicating all things wedding.

"Don't remind me. What was I thinking when I told my mom, yes, to shooting it for her? Ugh, weddings. Pain in the ass. She'll want specific shots more than candids." Trudy looked up and gave me the evil eye. "Don't look at me like that. You know I hate making a list of pictures. Mom and Dad, the wedding party, and on and on. People get bored waiting for the food and the fun to begin."

"Yeah, but it's her wedding, and she should have what she wants."

"You're so right, but it doesn't have to be me taking them. I wonder if I could find her someone else. I'd be willing to pay for a better wedding photographer than me."

"G'Anna. You're terrible. Cara is family. You should want to do this."

My heavy camera bag which I'd taken home last night to clean the lenses, slung around behind me when I hauled it off the table. "I know you're right, but ugh... I don't want to do this."

When my phone beeped, I walked to my workroom slash office. I glanced down to see Chandler's name on the screen followed by the text.

> **Chandler**: *Thought you were going to fly up with us.*

Setting the bag on the tabletop, I typed...

> **G'Anna**: *I planned to but decided to wait and join y'all a little later.*

It only took a second, and the phone rang. I knew Chandler wouldn't let it go.

"You could've flown with us on the private jet. Nothing like it in the world."

"I know, but I had some things to do this morning. The guys from Misunderstood wanted a consult about shooting the cover for their new EP."

"That's fantastic. Should be a piece of cake if you get them all in one place, not playing music, and sober."

I laughed knowing she spoke the truth. "Yeah, they haven't outgrown their band childhood. Banging, booze, and bitches." We both laughed.

"Yeah, I'm sure I'll get my fill of that before we get off tour. Carter and Gunner plan to whore their way across Europe when we go."

"TMI, I don't need to hear about those two. Now I'm going to think about it every time I look through the lens at them."

Chandler's loud laugh made me move the phone back from my ear. Dropping it on the table, I turned on the speaker. "Better than me. I have to witness it at every stop."

"True. Sorry. At least they're pleasant to look at." These guys were too hot for their own good. They put the S in sex with their perfect bodies and drop-dead gorgeous faces.

I'd seen them shirtless more than once and knew how wild the women went when they stripped down at the end of a set to throw the sweat-drenched fabric at the audience. More than once, it almost caused a fight, and I stood too close for comfort with my cameras dangling around my neck.

"Eww. I don't even want to talk about that. I've also seen a lot of other things they do living on the bus with them. Believe me when I say, you don't want pictures."

"Oh, right. Like having all that testosterone around twenty-four-seven is such a hardship."

"All I can say is sweaty bodies confined to a bus isn't something to get excited over."

"Well, I'd take your place, but they'd look at me like I was their mother, and that would only make me feel old."

"You're not old. Everyone in Steel is older than you and look how much their bodies still light up an audience. The women go crazy for those guys just as much as the young ones in Assured Distraction."

"True. I guess I don't think about the members of Steel being around my age."

"Yeah, and look at Ryder. More flying panties land around his feet than Keeton dreams of, or used to."

Remarks from people in the background filtered through her phone and across my speaker. I laughed at whichever band member made the noises.

"Shut up. No one wants to see hot pink, double D bras landing at their mic stand, Carter," Chandler chastised the bass player. I knew he had a smartass comeback for her, but the words met her fingers covering the phone mic. "Anyway, G'Anna. We'll see you soon, then?"

"Sure, I'll be there ready to go tomorrow." I glanced at Trudy and raised my eyebrows. She shrugged her shoulders confirming I should be able to get there by then before saying my goodbyes.

The studio where I'd planned to meet the new clients wasn't too far from my office. The young guys sat around in the lounge playing on their phones when I stepped through the doorway.

"Hello. I'm G'Anna Lucian. I'm supposed to have an appointment with Misunderstood about photos." They all looked up at me, but only one stood and spoke.

"Hey, I'm Britton, the lead singer and spokesman for the band." He shook my hand briefly.

As we shook, I looked him closely in the face. This band appeared barely out of diapers. I wonder if they realize how much I charge for a shoot. Surely, Trudy told them all about the fees when she booked this appointment.

"Ms. Lucian, we need to have a great photo to use for our cover. Your name came up over and over when we asked around, so I'm assuming you specialize in that."

"My photos cross many lines of the photography business, but yes, I've shot many bands before. If you looked at my work online, you've seen how many album covers I've done and how many magazine covers I've taken of bands."

"Right." He pointed his finger at me like it was a gun and clicked his tongue. Cocky much?

"We've brainstormed ideas about how we want it shot already and are prepared to discuss them with you today." He turned and looked at the other guys and jerked his head sideways indicating they needed to join us at the only table in the room. He held out his hand in its direction. "Please, join us."

I walked to the table, and he pulled out my chair. At least someone tried to teach him manners. "Okay. Let me start by saying timing is going to be tight for me. I'm leaving on a four-month European tour with a band. I'll be back in three months for a brief visit to fulfill a family obligation."

"And you're leaving when?" Britton asked. His tone told me immediately he was displeased with what I'd already said.

"Actually, I'm leaving as soon as we're done. The band is playing a couple of shows in New York and want me there tonight to capture the first one."

"Hmmm… interesting." He looked down at the table. "Is this Assured Distraction and Steel?"

I usually didn't share the finer points of my schedule with clients, but the well-advertised concert wasn't a secret. "Yes, it is."

"So, from what you're saying, I'm assuming you're starting their big Euro tour with them when you leave." He cocked an eyebrow.

Right away, I knew this shoot wouldn't happen. I didn't like his attitude or smartass comments. Answering to this kid wasn't my style.

"Well?" he continued with the inquiry.

"Look, Britton…" I started folding my calendar and papers back together. This interrogation was over. "I don't think I'm the right person to do your cover shot. Our styles don't click. Your band needs to find someone else. If you'd like a recommendation for someone who will do a fantastic job for you, call my office and talk to my secretary."

He stood so fast his chair fell over backward causing all the other members to stand, too. Looking around, I jumped to my feet. Intimidation tactics never worked with me.

Ryder Steel

"Not so fast, Ms. Lucian, please." He took in a breath. "We only want the best to take the picture, and we both know it's you. So, let's not get ahead of ourselves here."

I spun around and headed for the door. "No, Britton. I'm not getting ahead, I'm getting out. Find another photographer. I'm not interested in shooting your band."

"Oh, I suppose because you're old, and we're young, you think you can make decisions for us?"

I looked at him as I opened the door. "Your age has nothing to do with this. It's your attitude. I'd never work with someone as cocky as you. And for the record... I don't take suggestions for shots from bands, they take direction from me. You might not want to lead with a comment like that with the next sucker you find."

He stuck his gun finger back out and made the same clicking noise. "We'll keep that in mind, but I think you'll change your mind and do the job. For now, go hang out with your old men. They're has-beens anyway."

Laughter escaped my lips before I could get out the door fast enough. "Little shit's gotta lot to learn," I said to myself as I walked to the building's exit door.

Page | **65**

I scrolled through my emails standing outside JFK in New York City waiting on my Uber. The trunk popped open scaring me enough to pull my attention up in time to see the driver running around to load my suitcase.

"You keeping the backpack?"

"Oh yeah, sure." I looked up again and acknowledged he'd spoken to me. Staring at my phone in this big city was probably a bad plan. I needed to be more aware of what was going on around me.

A new car smell hit me when I climbed into the back seat. It didn't look new, but it had that fragrance associated with one. "Madison Square Gardens, please."

"Right. It's on my phone."

"Sorry, right. I forget it's not a cab." I looked up at the front dash to see if any identification might be displayed. Some cities required it. Apparently, New York City wasn't one of them.

"Going to see something good there?" The driver made some idle conversation as we began the traffic-laden route.

"Yes, I'm going to catch Steel's concert tonight."

"Getting there kinda' early, aren't you?"

Divulging that expensive camera equipment rode in my bags never seemed like a good plan, so I never said what I did. "Oh, uh... yeah. I'm meeting a friend there to go to dinner first." He nodded his head accepting the information. I knew they were instructed to make conversation for better ratings, so I played along with his list of impersonal questions about the city until we arrived at the enormous venue.

"Thank you." His tip slid from my fingers to his.

He smiled since people usually included tips on the app. "You bet. Enjoy your show tonight. Steel's one of my favorite bands. I've seen a couple of their shows before."

"Good to know." My rolling bag waited for my attention with the handle extended, so I grabbed it and started toward the guard sitting on a stool at the gate. He kept random people from going where the buses parked in the back of the venue.

"Yeah?" He looked me up and down.

"I'm G'Anna Lucian. I have an appointment with the two bands performing tonight."

"Right. I need some ID and to hear from the band. They didn't leave me any instructions for someone coming in." He took my driver's license and pass from me.

"Okay, I'll call them."

RYDER

Sitting around backstage always bored me to tears. Now we were going back out on tour, I quickly realized my feelings hadn't changed.

One of the roadies walked through the green room where we waited. "Zeke, can you get me my Gibson? I feel like writing a little music."

"Sure thing. I'm headed back out there in a sec." He made a pass by the food provided by the caterers snagging a couple of sandwiches.

Joel finally sat up on the opposite couch where he'd slept for over an hour. "You're gonna write? Dude, it's been a long time."

"Yeah, but I've been carrying around some music in my head for a while now. I'm ready to put it down on paper. Care to join me?"

"Hell yeah, I'll join. You know I fucking love writing new tunes."

The door opened with Zeke walking through carrying two acoustic guitars. The instruments' age and abuse made them stick out like sore thumbs. We always used these to write the first versions of our songs.

Zeke handed them over. "I figured if Ryder were writing, you'd be joining him. So I brought yours, too."

"Thanks, Zeke-man. You know us too well." The two bumped fists.

"I should after all the years I've been traveling with y'all."

"Shut up, fucker. You make me feel old."

"Then guess how old I feel when y'all bring the next generation on tour with us? Feels like I've lived a thousand lives in twenty years."

"I damn sure do, too. You should be one of 'em's dad. That'll really make you feel ancient," I added.

"Both of you shut up. I'm not old." Joel strummed across the strings. "I'm seasoned. Just think of all we know now that we didn't know at their age."

Ryder Steel

"Yeah, and it's up to us to show them what not to be so stupid about. I expect you not to act like the douchebag you were when we were their age, please."

Zeke shook his head laughing on the way back out. "Yeah, I'm gonna hold my breath on that one." The door slammed behind him.

"So, new music. Let's hear what you got."

I began playing the opening riff I'd been tossing around in my head. I knew Joel would love it. He always enjoyed beginning with this type of intro. Made for a perfect start to a show. Play a riff that the audience recognized, and it would send them into a frenzy before the lights illuminated the band.

I played through the intro, the first verse, and down to the chorus before stopping. I turned to Joel. "Well, what do you think?"

"What do I think? I think I fucking love it. It's our next top ten. That's what I think. Why you been holding off on letting anyone hear it?" He began picking out the rhythm on his guitar. "Let's hear the rest."

Before I could say anything, the door opened. Chandler walked in followed by the hot little photographer friend of hers. Chandler told us she would be around for our gigs to take some pictures, but I didn't realize she was shooting us in the U.S.

Thia Finn

"Oh, hey, Ryder. Joel. This is my friend and the official photog for the tour, G'Anna Lucian."

Both of us set aside our guitars and stood. Her small hand fit into mine like a glove, and I swore I felt an immediate connection between us. It must have been from knowing she was the first friend of my daughter's for me to officially meet.

"Hello. It's great to finally meet one of Chandler's friends." I pumped her hand longer than needed, but I couldn't bring myself to let her go until Joel made a noise. I immediately pulled my hand back only for Joel to pick hers up and shake it briefly.

"Nice to meet you, G'Anna. Great name, by the way," he added.

"It's wonderful to meet you both." She beamed a beautiful smile at us. She looked at Joel. "And thank you. My parents are from Italy, but I was born here."

"Sweet, a full-blooded Italian woman. I bet you can cook like a dream. Do you speak Italian, too?" Joel openly flirted with this gorgeous woman as I stood back and watched it all unfold.

I didn't flirt. I hardly carried on conversations with women. It's not like I didn't speak to women. We had some with our roadie team from time to time, especially with the sound people. I talked to them about what I wanted changed. I gave suggestions or

Page | 72

requests, and they completed them. I spoke, they listened.

This was different. This was holding a polite conversation. I didn't spend time doing much that would be considered polite. Thinking about it, I realized I couldn't remember the last time I engaged in polite conversation with a female.

If I wanted a woman for the night, someone arranged it. We fucked. I slept. Someone escorted her out before morning. That's the way I wanted it. I didn't need to find a connection with a woman after Laina. The soft sound of G'Anna's voice brought me out of my thoughts.

"You'd be sadly disappointed if you tasted anything I attempted to cook, Italian or otherwise. I leave the cooking to my mother. But, I can cuss like a sailor in Italian. That's about the extent of my foreign language." Laughter broke out among the group at her admission.

"Sounds like I'll have to make you mad so I can hear your best skills then," Joel jokingly told our new acquaintance as I sat back and watched the banter between them. It easily flowed for them, and for the first time in forever, I felt jealous of Joel's ability to strike up a conversation on the fly this way.

I hadn't considered my lack of conversation with a beautiful woman. Thinking back, I couldn't remember a single time I'd conversed with a female other than a relative in forever. Damn, I needed to do something about this. Here I stood with my daughter and her gorgeous friend with nothing to say, nothing of interest to add to the light flirting Joel engaged them with. God, I was fucking lame even to myself.

"So, Dad..." Chandler turned to me bringing me out of my head, "... I thought if G'Anna could arrange her schedule, she might travel with us for a few days here in the U.S. and shoot some action pictures to use on social media or maybe for later in a video. Would you be okay with that?"

"Sure, Chandler. Whatever you want is fine with me." I moved around beside her and captured her shoulder pulling her into my side. "If you're happy, I'm happy."

G'Anna spoke up. "Wow. Chandler, it's the perfect opportunity to go wild with that kind of answer. Can you sneak dear ol' Dad's credit card for the afternoon? We can do some serious damage." The little minx looked at me and winked. How was I supposed to react to that? Did she look at me like an old man because Chandler was my daughter?

Ryder Steel

"She can have her own card to my account. I'll set it up with a phone call." I pulled my cell out of my back pocket.

"No. No. No." Chandler pushed my hand down. "I don't need anything, and besides, I have plenty of my own money."

"Yeah, but I've never had the chance to let you have a free day of shopping on me." I'd missed so much of Chandler's growing up, I wanted to make up for lost time any way I could.

"Thank you." She kissed me on the cheek. "I'll keep that in mind when I'm ready to go. Today's not the day, though. We've got too much to do." She turned to G'Anna. "Besides, we're going to be in Paris soon. We can do some serious damage over there."

"Absolutely," the photographer added in a fake French accent. "Let's put a day off on the calendar, so we don't miss out. *Champs-Élysées* here we come."

The two air-kissed each cheek directly in front of me. A light fragrance of lavender caught my attention when G'Anna leaned into my daughter. My senses perked up and went straight down my body causing my dick to twitch. Dammit, I was too old to let one feminine fragrance cause my dick to act fourteen again. Maybe she was right to consider me an old

Page | 75

man. Guess that ship had sailed for me with a woman like her.

G'ANNA

I stood in front of the stage and shot photos nonstop while Steel's music drove the crowd wild. Every member performed as though it could be their last show and wanted it to be their best. They played to the audience's roar of praise and singing the lyrics of the songs they knew so well. The connection the band shared with the audience caused goosebumps on my arms. Devotion of this nature could only be earned over time.

The pictures taken when Assured Distraction opened for Steel from the same spot proved the audience loved them. But, when the initial strum from Ryder's guitar came across the speaker, the praise moved past love. Adoration better described the audience's vibe. I watched the band create this passion in the fans bouncing around me until I was caught up in it as well.

Ryder Steel brought out other feelings inside me, though. I had to face it. The man was freaking hot. His trimmed beard helped define a perfect face. I knew he'd worn his hair longer in the early days of Steel, but now he kept the sides shorn close, and the top did its own thing. The salt and pepper locks curled loosely and moved around to the beat going through Ryder's body to the music he pulled from his guitar.

The denim-snapped shirt hugged his trim body in a custom fit that I knew he commissioned. Anyone who made the kind of money Steel did surely wore clothes made to their specifications, just like the torn jeans he always had on. Heavy black boots that tapped out the rhythm the music followed finished out his stage clothes.

Lifting my camera once again, I adjusted the settings to capture a natural pose on the lead singer and his guitar. As I snapped off a slew of him, I noticed he'd turned his head and was looking directly at me. I pulled the camera away from my face and met his gaze. A brief smile grazed his mouth, and he directed it at me while he continued singing about love and loss. We seemed to be stuck in time while the song played on, his lyrics coming from rote memory as we remained connected.

"He's got a thing for you." A nudge from the photographer standing next to me caused me to break my stare.

"What? No." My head shook back and forth.

"He sang that entire song to you. Bitch, he's hot. I'd do him in a heartbeat." She gave me a knowing look before turning back to her viewfinder.

I watched her shoot for a minute trying to think of a comeback to her comment. It never happened, though. She was clearly mistaken. He only looked in my direction because he knew I was shooting pictures for later use. Ryder Steel wouldn't give me a second thought. He barely spoke to me when I'd met him earlier today.

Raising my camera back to stage level, I took pictures of the rest of the band and their antics for the remainder of their set. Steel knew how to entertain their audience, and they did so for close to two full hours.

Shortly before the last song started, I made my way to the side of the stage. Chandler and KeeMac were watching in the wings, and she spotted me standing in front of two security guards blocking the way. A brief nod between us told me she knew I'd wait until the last note faded before trying to get back to them.

When the band made their way offstage following the second encore, Ryder spotted me and crooked his finger. I tapped the guard and pointed to Ryder who made the motion again. Both men stepped apart allowing me to go up the steps. Ryder didn't wait for me, but when I got to the top, Joel grabbed my hand and led me offstage. The audience's cheers made talking impossible. They begged for a third encore, but it wouldn't happen.

"That was insane." Chandler nodded her head in response. "I've been to lots of concerts but never have I felt like the audience, and the band connected the way they did tonight."

"Yeah, one day, we'll have fans like Steel does. Right, babe?" She wrapped her arm around KeeMac's waist, and he leaned down and kissed her.

"You're fucking right we will. I can feel it happening with each venue we play."

"Keeton's always the optimist about our success." Chandler's smile at him expressed the love they strongly shared.

We made our way back to a conference room backstage where a meet-and-greet, photos with the fans, and autographs had been staged. I lifted my

Ryder Steel

camera and looked through the viewfinder at some possible shots with both bands and their fans. Having attended these occasionally, I knew what to expect, but the aggressiveness of the Steel fans shocked me.

From a vantage point behind Chandler, I watched women basically try to strip for Steel's members to capture their attention. When a pair of double D's almost unfolded on Ryder's face, I let out a squeal causing him to look over at me. He smiled and shrugged his shoulders as he wrote his name across the bare flesh. I shook my head in disbelief.

"Is this what I can expect at all the venues?" I whispered in Chandler's ear.

"Oh that? Yeah, they're bold, aren't they? Some skanky ones manage to get tickets no matter how hard the PR people try to keep it from happening."

KeeMac started laughing at her description of the woman who now turned to show off her signed boobs.

"Thank God there are no children in here," I told the couple.

"Children aren't allowed backstage, ever, after a show," Chandler said aloud so the fans could hear it. I guess she wanted everyone to know behavior like that woman's wouldn't be tolerated with kids around.

"Good to know." I slipped around behind the tables where Steel sat so I might capture other angles of their interaction with the fans. As I made my way behind Ryder, he glanced back at me and smiled.

"Did you enjoy the show?"

"You know it. Your fans are amazing." I focused on the next woman leaning down to talk to Ryder.

"Yeah, they are, aren't they?" He turned and asked the woman her name before signing the poster she laid in front of him. When she walked on down the line, he looked at me again. "Do you want to sit here with us? Uh... I mean, you can get another perspective from being in the middle of this madness."

I didn't have to be asked twice to sit between Ryder and Jason, their keyboard player. He was every bit as great to look at as Ryder, and I'd yet to speak to him directly.

I stuck my hand out. "Hello, G'Anna Lucian. We've not been introduced."

He took my hand in both of his and shook it. "Very nice to meet you, G'Anna. How come Chandler's been keeping you hidden from us?" He wiggled his eyebrows at me.

I couldn't help laughing out loud. "Uh... I don't know."

"Maybe it's because she knew you'd be acting like a total dick to our photographer from the minute you met her," Ryder said leaning over in front of me to address Jason. "Now play nice. She's going to be with us in Europe most of the time."

"Even better. Lots of romantic places to wine and dine a beautiful woman in Europe." I tugged my hand from his and looked up at the next scantily clad female staring at the two men.

"I believe this lady wants an autograph, guys."

"Hell yeah, I do. I'd be willing to trade for more than that." She winked at Ryder and smiled at Jason.

"Uh... right. I think we're leaving as soon as this is over tonight," Ryder informed the brazen young woman.

I sat back and watched the twenty-something shamelessly flirt with the two rockers who leaned over to sign the photo page. Her forwardness shocked me some because she was a gorgeous blonde. Her tall, willowy body looked made for the runway. Why would she need to act this way to men so much older than she was? Surely, she rarely found herself needing a date.

I lifted my camera as she scooted closer to the table. I wanted to capture her natural beauty, but when she ripped her fishnet stockings so close to her panties, I stared over the top of the lens.

"Why don't you guys sign here? It'll be so much more memorable." The blonde looked up at me. "You can get a picture for them to remember me by."

I swallowed with a gulp. "Uh... sure. If that's what they want."

Jason jumped up grabbing his *Sharpie*. "Hell yeah. Let's do this." He leaned over the table, and she hiked up her tiny skirt, so the hot pink, see-through panties showed him her bare pussy. His position had him up close and personal with her smooth skin. "Well, well," whispered from his lips to hers.

My mouth fell open as I stared at the scene in front of me. I couldn't have taken a clearer picture if I'd tried. While he signed the spot on her upper thigh, the woman ran her hand down his back to the skin showing between his jeans and t-shirt. She slid her fingernail across the space on his lower back slowly and deep enough to get his attention. He didn't rise up from the table until she put her room key in his back pocket.

"I'm Ellie, and my room number's on the key."

Jason stood and nodded his head and looked around. "Nice to meet you, Ellie. See you in an hour or so." He stuck his hand out to the next person in line effectively dismissing her.

Ryder Steel

"Close your mouth, G'Anna." I felt his palm on my chin.

"Wh... What?" Steel turned my head to look at him.

"You need to close your mouth or people will be looking at you like you were looking at her." I felt his hand move away from my skin and immediately was disappointed. Every time he touched me, I felt a tingle in my skin.

"That was unbelievable. Is it always like this?"

Ryder nodded his head affirming the answer. "Happens at least once, but usually it's several times. Let us have an after party, and the groupies get more brazen than you'll ever want to see. Chandler can probably tell you some stories to make that perfect hair of yours stand on end." He stared at me a moment as if trying to send me more information telepathically. "You might want to close your mouth again." He laughed and picked up his pen.

The rest of the signing seemed tame compared to what I'd seen, but I kept my eyes open and my mouth shut until the last fan took a picture with Daniel and Joel. I looked across and saw the Assured Distraction gang thanking the radio hosts who'd planned the event.

Getting back to my hotel room so these guys could do whatever they had planned was my first priority. I didn't want to intrude on their private time or make them feel like they needed to include me. More pictures than I bargained for sat waiting on my camera, with plenty of shots and a world of insight into a rock band's signing autographs.

RYDER

Before I could pick up my water bottle and turn to speak to G'Anna, she'd made her way around to the other side of the room. I guessed she'd had enough of hanging out with me for the night. I wasn't through hanging out with her, though.

"We're going back to the hotel and ordering room service, Ryder. I'm starving." The look KeeMac gave to Chandler told me they starved for more than food. This type of relationship took some getting used to. The other band members I had no problems with, but the way he and Chandler lusted after each other still bothered me.

I looked over at the woman I felt an unusual attraction to. Her natural beauty and the easy way she carried herself captured my attention.

"G'Anna, you have plans for the rest of the evening?" Chandler called across the room. It surprised me, but when I looked at my daughter, she had a knowing smirk on her lips.

Before G'Anna got back to us, I asked, "Are you hungry? We can go get some dinner if you'd like."

She looked at the two lovers and then back at me. "I don't want to intrude on your dinner."

"You're not intruding. I'm inviting you to have dinner with me." I needed it to be clear this was me asking her to go. I watched her reaction to see if she wanted to or was simply being polite.

"Uh... sure. If you don't mind me tagging along." From the look on her face, I believed she wanted to have dinner with me. She turned back to Chandler. "I'm sure you two are welcome to join us."

KeeMac spoke up, "Nope. Got other things to take care of." He pulled Chandler's body flush with his. "Ain't that right, babe?"

If I had to guess, he was already sporting a hard-on between them, and that was something I didn't need to see. The man-child roamed around in his underwear or naked from time to time. I'd seen enough of him than necessary more than once and had told him so.

"Oh, right. Okay." G'Anna looked at me. "Guess it's just the two of us then."

"Well, we both know it won't be Jason." I laughed so hard at the look on her face. KeeMac and Chandler glanced between the two of us. "G'Anna here had the pleasure of watching one of the groupies in action at our table. I believe she was sufficiently indoctrinated to the groupie way of doing things."

"Oh God," Chandler commented. "What did the skank do?"

I took G'Anna by the elbow and led her toward the doorway where security stood waiting. Over my shoulder, I added, "Use your imagination." When I looked up, G'Anna's face was glowing red. It'd been a long time since I'd made a woman blush. This might be an interesting night.

The massive SUV pulled in front of an all-night diner where I knew we'd be served good food. Being on the road for so long, we had places located in every city which served food until late or all night. "Sorry about our choice of places, but at this hour, you're subject to what's still open. The good news is, the food's excellent, and it's usually empty this time of night."

"I'm sure it's fine. Great even, if you guys eat here."

"Ha. We've eaten at every dump and dive from coast to coast. We could do our own *Diners, Drive-ins, and Dives* show. Fieri's got nothing on Steel, except we've eaten at the bad ones, too."

Security went in ahead of us and signaled for us to enter. "I'm sorry we have to have these guys with us, too, but we don't go anywhere without them for our safety. People can be crazy sometimes and do stupid stuff that they'll regret later in life."

"Bet you've seen it all."

Taking her elbow again, we moved to the back booth, and I sat with my back to the doorway. My guy would stop anyone from coming to our table, but there were only a few all-night workers and a cop sitting in the place.

"Hope you're hungry because I'm starving after a show."

"I could eat something." She looked over the menu. When the young waitress made her way to us, G'Anna spoke up, "I'll have a bacon cheeseburger with all the trimmings and an order of French fries with a chocolate shake."

The waitress stopped writing, staring at my companion before looking at me. "I'll have the same, except I'll have a strawberry shake." She gave me a bored nod and walked away. "I love a girl not afraid to eat when she's hungry." We both laughed.

"Eating's never been a problem for me, but I don't eat this late very often."

It was going to be necessary for me to talk this time. With only the two of us at the table, I had to step up my game. I hoped I remembered how to do this.

G'Anna caught me off guard when she commented first. "I just want to know one thing, Ryder."

"What's that?" I needed to be attentive, so I met her gaze. Her brown eyes reminded me of a mink coat. The iris didn't seem uniform in color but held an array of browns as I'd seen in a coat, some dark, some light. Against her olive skin and the black hair that fanned her face, they captured my attention and held it.

"Do all of the band members get that kind of aggressiveness from groupies like I witnessed tonight?"

I chuckled as the waitress set our frosty drinks down in front of us. Once she moved far enough away from the table, I looked back at G'Anna still waiting for an answer. "Yeah, we've all been treated to those types of women and even a few men. None of us swing that way, but it's still happened."

"So, you've come to expect behavior like that from women at every show?" G'Anna opened her straw and took a long drink of the decadent chocolate.

"Yeah, we have. I guess we're jaded to most things after all this time of touring. Some women will do anything to say they've slept with a rock star."

"Oh, so that's how it is? All the Mr. Rock Gods like the idea of getting to choose a different woman every night?" She smiled as she said it, but her tone said sarcasm.

"We still get women hitting on us, but the truth is, we rarely take them up on it. Jason and his longtime girlfriend broke up a few months ago, and he's gotten back into the manwhoring. The rest of the band are married with kids or been with the same woman for years, and they have families."

"And what about Ryder Steel? Where does he fall into these categories?"

I knew we would be discussing my life at some point, but I didn't realize we would jump right into it so quickly.

When I failed to answer immediately, G'Anna spoke up, "I'm sorry. Don't answer that. It's none of my business. Really, I didn't mean to pry into your personal life. I'm sorry."

I reached out and took her hand off the table. "It's okay. I'm surprised Chandler hasn't told you this already." She looked at me and barely shook her head no. "You know she's my daughter. Her mom and I were together long before she was born… high school sweethearts. I didn't know her mom was pregnant when I left on tour. By the time I finally found out, her mom was gone, disappeared from my life. I never knew about my baby girl until Chandler came looking for me this year. Being a dad is all new to me."

"Oh, Ryder. I'm so sorry. I only knew she was your daughter, not the other details."

"Nothing for you to be sorry about. We're just getting acquainted. I wanted them on tour with us, so I could get to know her better and spend time with her."

"That all had to be hard on you… the not knowing."

"I'm not going to lie. It's been hell, but we're working on having a relationship, and I believe it's going pretty well. Of course, she has KeeMac, who also wants a lot of her time as I do." We both laughed. "He doesn't make any bones about what he wants with her. They're newly in love and all."

"Yeah, that's easy to tell. They can't keep their hands off of each other." As soon as she said it, she looked at me. "Oh sorry. That's your daughter we're talking about."

"Don't I know it. Their whole relationship is a bitter pill to swallow. I've lived his life already. He's so much like I was at his age. I know the adrenaline high they feel coming off stage. I suppose the good thing is they have each other and aren't taking strangers to bed after every show like we did back in those days."

"Good to know. I'll do my best to avoid them and the other band members after a show." I smiled at her, and she laughed. "The last thing I want to do is put a kink in their plans."

He cringed. "Don't say kink, please." We both laughed again. "They'll get it out of their system quickly. That life gets old too fast."

"I can only imagine." I stared at her wondering what she imagined about our lifestyles. She's in a business that deals with creative people daily. Surely, she'd seen it all with models, bands, and the like.

"So, tell me, G'Anna, has photography always been in your blood?"

She ran her finger up and down the sweating glass. Whether she realized it or not, the movement created a sensual look. The slow slide up and down taking the moisture with her only to have it roll over the top of her finger when it got to be too heavy gave me all kinds of dirty ideas.

I watched it thinking about how that would look if it was my cock she ran a finger up and down. A familiar stir began behind my zipper. It'd been a long while since I'd had a woman lying in bed with me enjoying languid pleasures between us. I dragged my eyes back to hers and found her staring at me.

She quickly moved her hand to the napkin wiping away the water. "My parents gave me a camera for Christmas after months of begging for one when I was ten. I'd gone on a field trip to the art museum, and an entire floor was a show of famous photographers. You know like *Dorothea Lange, Robert Capa*, and, of course, *Ansel Adams.*

"The masters are great, but I needed more action so when I got old enough to start appreciating music, I found photographers who shot bands. Now I fangirl over shots by people like *Todd Owyoung* and *Valerio Berdini*. I've followed their careers since they became well-known. They're not much older than I am, though."

I watched her talk about these guys with such enthusiasm. I'd only heard of a few of these photographers. That side of the industry came with the label. Between them and our manager, all of it was taken care of. I rarely ever gave it much thought but seeing it through her eyes, it became obvious she studied her craft. I could only equate it to me studying *Hendrix* or *Townsend* or even *Stevie Ray Vaughan.*

"Oh, sorry. Guess I got carried away. Talking about photography gets me excited."

"I can tell." I chuckled a little. "I completely get it, though. I'm the same way when you start talking about musicians."

"So, you study their work?"

"Well, their styles. The sounds they can pull from a guitar amazes me." I looked up. "You know exactly what I mean?"

"Yeah, I do."

We both stared at each other lost in our own world of excellence in our craft. The waitress finally broke the silence which was a relief to me. She set our food down and walked away without saying a word. I followed her movement wondering how she kept a job.

"Talkative thing, huh?" I uttered making G'Anna laugh.

"Yeah, bet she's bankrolled with those amazing tips she takes home." I nodded before taking a bite. I felt like we didn't have to make pretentious conversation to pass the time.

Ryder Steel

We paid our bill and walked out to the open door of the SUV waiting to take us back to the hotel. With my hand at the small of her back, I led her to the open door. As the car pulled away, I missed the connection of touching her. I reached for her hand, and she let me hold it. Sharing this warmth with her felt perfect to me. I hoped she had the same reaction to it.

G'ANNA

Where was my head at? Holding hands like teenagers? Was this a thing for him? Did he need a constant connection? Maybe I read more into it than he did.

I hadn't dated in a while. I never had time anymore with my life constantly scheduled and on the go. As the vehicle made its way through the narrow streets of New York, I thought back to the last time I'd gone to dinner with a man. It had been a long time, and even longer since I'd had sex with something not rubber or plastic.

Not that I'd be having sex with Ryder. No, far from it. This was a friendly dinner after a big show. He wanted to dine with a friend. I know he could have easily found a female companion anytime he wanted it. He said as much, but instead, he asked me. Maybe he wanted a friend and fuck buddy tonight.

"You're quiet. Is everything okay?" His soft voice the total opposite of the volume he left behind on stage.

"Yeah, everything's great. Thank you for dinner. I appreciate you inviting me. I'd have probably skipped it altogether and had a candy bar and diet soda from the vending machine."

"That's no way for an adult to eat."

"Oh, so cheeseburgers, fries, and shakes are higher in the food hierarchy?"

"Well, when you put it like that, I guess a Coke and candy bar doesn't sound so bad."

I caught a smile on his lips as we passed under the streetlight. "I'm glad you said yes to coming with me. I don't get to take beautiful women to a quiet dinner very often."

"Now you're talking crazy. You and I both know you could easily take supermodels to dinner whenever you wanted."

"The truth is, I can't tell you the last time I had a date. We've drifted around the world so much. When we're home, we spend our time writing music. The guys have families. Hell, I don't even own a home."

This shocked me. "What do you mean? Where do you live?"

"Hotels, mostly. Sometimes I'll stay at one of the guys' homes."

"Where do you keep your stuff?"

"Stuff?" I could tell he didn't have a clue.

"You know, your things, furniture, mementos, pots, and pans." He laughed at me.

"G'Anna, I don't have stuff. What I own fits in a few suitcases. What doesn't fit there is in a warehouse in Austin. They load it in and out when we leave on tour. Someone else sees to it. They buy what I want for the tour and have it where we show up."

The car came to a stop behind the hotel. Ryder's security team opened the door, so the wild information he'd shared with me ended abruptly. I filed it away for a later date, though. Who lived that way?

Reaching the doorway of my room, I pulled the key out, and he took it from me to open the door. I had a regular hotel room, nothing special. He looked in and turned to me. "Uh... you want to go to my suite? We can have some coffee or champagne or something."

I knew he'd been in rehab from his early days. That information was public knowledge. I didn't know if he drank now or not. Once an addict, always an addict, or so I'd always been told.

My empty room didn't appear appealing to me either, so I pulled the door shut and took my key from his hand depositing it back in my purse. "Sounds good to me." We started toward the elevator that security held open.

Of course, he was in the penthouse on the top floor. When security opened the door, and I walked through, the view from all the opened drapes took my breath away. The living area opened on two sides with an opulent view of the city.

"Wow, Ryder. This is unbelievable. The city looks beautiful from here." He walked beside me and looked out.

"I guess it does. I usually stay in this room when I'm in New York. Guess I haven't paid much attention to it in a while."

"How could you not?" I moved to the other set of windows looking at a different part of Manhattan. "It's a perfect view of the city. I love it."

"Move in here then. There's more than enough rooms. Of course, you have to put up with KeeMac since they stay with me. You can have my room. I hardly sleep anymore anyway."

Page | **101**

I turned away from the lights and looked at him. "Are you out of your mind? I couldn't ask you to move from your bedroom so I could sleep here. Besides, I already have a room. Downstairs, remember? The one with the view of the parking garage?"

He pulled his cell from his pocket and hit a button. The door opened, and the same security guy walked in. "Yes, Mr. Steel?"

"Please have the Miss Lucian's things moved here from her room downstairs."

"Yes, sir." Before I could protest, the man disappeared.

"No, no, no. I can't just move in here with you guys."

"Why not?" He looked at me as though he truly didn't understand.

"Ryder, it's a generous offer, but I'm fine in my room."

"Then you'll be fine in a room here, too."

"I can't share a room with you." My voice was almost at screeching level.

"You're not sharing a room with me." He moved toward a door on the opposite side of the room. When I didn't follow, he turned back. "Come on before Sam gets here with your luggage."

"I'll look, but I'm not staying here. I need my personal space, and the room I have booked is perfect for me."

"We'll see." He nodded toward the open doorway.

My hesitant steps to the bedroom stopped at the door. The floor-to-ceiling windows overlooked Central Park. This had to be the master suite. While I went to the windows to look out, Ryder walked to the ensuite and flipped the light switch drawing my attention to it. The brightness captured my attention, so I decided to check it out first. When I stepped through the door, all I saw was white elegance. I'd never seen anything like it before. The walk-in tub was built for more than one, as was the huge all-glass shower standing behind it. But what held my attention were the floor-to-ceiling windows.

"Uh... it's kinda open, isn't it?" I gestured to the window.

"You'd think that, but you'd be wrong. The windows are made so you can only see out. No one can see in unless you want them to." He reached back and flipped a switch, and the color of them changed. "Now they can see you in here."

"Who would want that?" I knew my face must have looked ridiculous to him.

Thia Finn

"You know, G'Anna, some people are into that kind of thing. They enjoy people watching them, especially while they are having sex." His eyebrows raised up as though he waited for me to catch on to what he was saying.

"Oh, uh… yeah. I guess you're right." My face felt as red hot as it looked when I turned to the mirrors behind me. I wasn't naïve, but I never considered rooms would be made for voyeurism in an expensive hotel.

"I take it you're not one who enjoys people watching." He laughed as he put his arm around my shoulders and led me back to the bedroom area. White with silver-gray accents decorated the sleeping area with luxury written all over it before we stepped back into the common area.

"Not so much." I moved to one of the stark-white couches and curled up in a corner. "I'm still not staying here."

He hung his head. "I don't get it. Most women would have been sold the moment they stepped in the room and absolutely after seeing the bath."

"The room is beautiful and the bath to die for, but I'm happy in my room. Thank you, though."

Ryder tapped on his phone again. I guessed he was canceling the order to move my things since they never appeared at the door.

"What can I get you to drink? It's fully stocked." He opened a wine fridge and pulled out two bottles. "Red or white or champagne?" He moved to another door and opened it to a stocked bar. "Or would you prefer something stronger?"

"What are you having?" I didn't want to drink alone.

"I think I'll have a glass of this Pinot." He pulled a wine opener from a drawer. I wondered if he opened it for me.

"If you'd rather have coffee, I'm good with that, too."

"No, I like a glass of wine on occasion. Do you want this or would you rather a red?"

"Pinot is fine with me." He delivered the healthy glasses to the couch and sat at the end of my knees from where my feet were pulled up under me. I took the glass, and he placed the empty hand on my leg close to my knee. His palm sat safely in a good location. Touching but not too familiar.

RYDER

God, how did I find myself with a gorgeous woman drinking wine in my hotel room? We'd talked and laughed while killing the bottle of wine. I limited out on two glasses, so we made them last before moving on to sparkling water. She never mentioned my addictions, so I didn't offer any information. I controlled my drinking since rehab, and drugs were off the table and had been for years. The band didn't even smoke pot in the legal states anymore. We'd outgrown smoking when kids started coming along for the others.

"Oh my God. Do you know what time it is?" G'Anna jumped up and moved to the windows. "Ryder, that's the sun coming up." She wheeled around and looked at me. "We've stayed up all night. I can't remember the last time I saw the sun coming up from being out all night."

I moved up behind her and wrapped her in my arms. "Shhh. Just enjoy it then." She put her arms over the top of mine, and we held on to each other as the rays peeked up over the horizon. New York City sunrises could be spectacular if the clouds cooperated, and this was one of those mornings.

The calming lavender fragrance still delighted me when I had her this close. Her height allowed her to rest her head against my shoulder and my face to lay against the side of hers. I enjoyed having her close. I held her in a lover's embrace while we watched the sky light up with gold projecting up from the horizon.

The event passed quickly, but we stood there until I felt her leaning into me and her breathing light and consistent. She'd fallen asleep in my arms. I gently scooped her up carrying her to the room darkened with the touch of a button. Lying her down on the luxurious comforter, she didn't move. I pulled the throw from the foot of the bed to keep her warm. Covering her with my body and using my heat to keep her warm sounded perfect in my head, but I wasn't sure G'Anna would see it that way when she woke.

I watched her roll to her side and tuck the pillow under her head before I snuck from the room. I stopped at the doorway and reconsidered crawling in the bed next to her and pulling her into my arms to sleep. The memory of sleeping with a woman I knew rested so far back in my mind, I could hardly recall the euphoria of the feeling. I stood and watched her another minute as I thought of a night long ago when love was part of my life.

Pulling the door shut, I moved to the couch and laid down. Laina's memories flooded my mind even after all this time. I closed my eyes trying to recall before falling into a restless sleep.

A wonderful aroma woke me. "Coffee?"

"Yeah, old man. Why are you sleeping here when you've got a perfectly good king-size bed in the other room?" KeeMac asked while standing at a silver coffee urn rolled in by room service as I slept.

"Do not call me old man." The raspy sound of my voice grated my ears.

Ryder Steel

"Eww. He wakes up grumpy, Chan. Better watch out." This damn kid woke up loud. I don't know what's worse, him or me.

Chandler walked in wrapped in a fluffy robe smelling freshly showered. "Morning, Dad. Don't pay attention to Keeton. He's always like that when he wakes up." She moved to KeeMac and kissed his cheek. "I still love him, though." KeeMac pulled her close to him in a firm hold. Chandler rested her cheek against his naked chest and looked around the room. "Why *did* you sleep in here? The beds are super comfy."

"Not that we did much sleeping, babe," KeeMac murmured a little too loudly.

"KeeMac," I growled. "What have I told you about TMI between you and my daughter?"

KeeMac laughed. "Sorry, Mr. Steel. You know I love her, though." He held Chandler tight as she struggled to get out of his arms.

"Keeton. Don't say things like that."

"You brought it up, not me." KeeMac let her go but swatted her ass with a sound smack.

"Owww. That hurt." Chandler moved over to the couch facing me.

"So, back to our question. What were you doing last night? We didn't hear you come in after your dinner with G'Anna."

Sharing my actions with the band was bad enough. Now I had to share it with my daughter, too? I started to say something when the door to my room opened. G'Anna stepped through it with mussed hair and wearing the same clothes from last night. Chandler looked at G'Anna, then KeeMac, then me and back at KeeMac before she spoke.

"Don't say a word." Chandler gave him a nasty look to obviously shut him up. It seems the guy had no filter most of the time. He needed one now because if he said one derogatory word to G'Anna, he'd deal with me and not his sweetheart.

"Oh, good morning, you all. Wait, is it still morning, and is there more coffee? I can't think before my first cup." G'Anna crossed the room to the cart and poured herself some while the three of us watched her.

"No, actually it's after one," KeeMac announced.

"Damn, I haven't checked in with my assistant today. She's going to be pissed." She picked up her cell and started typing. I looked at Chandler and KeeMac, who'd sat down beside his girl, daring either of them to make a comment or ask a question regarding the sleeping arrangements again.

KeeMac received my message and put his arm around Chandler. "What are we going to do today, babe? You have any plans before the show?"

"Not really. What about you since we don't have to do another sound check?"

"I got nothing." He pulled her close and kissed her temple. "I thought we might go to *La Perla*. The mothership is on Broadway in Soho, and then *Agent Provocateur* has a shop just a few blocks from here. It's close enough to walk."

G'Anna almost spit coffee all over the room. "And you know this, how?"

Chandler spoke up. "He loves them both. I swear he has a direct line to the closest shops so they can text him when new stuff comes in. Personally, I'd be happy wearing anything from the *VS* catalog, but he likes more lace and mesh."

G'Anna moved closer and sat down on the other end of the couch where I sat trying to contain my comments. Why did they insist on discussing intimate things when I happened to be around?

G'Anna couldn't let it go, though. "Damn, girl. You found a winner with this big guy. I'd be happy to have a man buying me such beautiful lingerie." She never looked at me while she spoke.

Thia Finn

"Hell yeah, she did. I know what women like." I wanted to slap the Cheshire cat grin off his big ugly face. He might as well have beat his fists on his chest. He looked over at me after he said it and knew exactly what I was thinking. "Babe, I think we're going to have to get our own suite from now on. Dear old Dad isn't appreciating anything I fucking say this morning."

"Hell no, I'm not. Let's see, you started with referring to all the sex you had, then moved to buying some fancy lingerie. How could I be happy?"

Chandler stuck out her bottom lip and crawled in KeeMac's lap wrapping her arms around his neck. "I don't want to move to our own room, Keeton. This is as close to family time as I get with Dad." She laid her head on his shoulder to drive home her wishes.

"Sorry, babe. We won't stay in separate rooms, and I'll try harder to keep my mouth under control when he's around. But, what we do behind that fucking bedroom door, all bets are off."

Chandler sat up and kissed his cheek. "Thank you."

"My God, son. You're such a pussy when it comes to her. She must have your man card in her billfold or is it just your balls?" I laughed at my own joke because the other three didn't find my comment funny at all.

"I thought it was a good compromise, Ryder. You should be happy they're both willing to do so. Relationships are built on compromise."

I turned and stared at G'Anna. "Is that right? And what did Chandler give up to get her way?"

"Well, I feel like she did it because she wants to be with you more often, so why are you questioning it at all?"

"Good save there. Answering a question with a question and steer away from the subject." I enjoyed the repartee with her, and she knew it since I couldn't keep from smiling when I spoke to her.

"True, I enjoy a good debate anytime you want to spar with me."

"No thank you. I know I'd lose against the likes of you and Chandler." Chandler busted out laughing.

"No doubt about that, G'Anna."

G'ANNA

I grabbed my purse off the huge, live edge, walnut dining table. "I need to get moving. I've yet to make it to my room, and there are some places I'd like to get a few shots off while I'm here in the city."

Everyone else stood with me. "Come on, babe. I need to show you something behind *our* bedroom door." KeeMac snickered as he said it and gave Ryder a head tip as he took Chandler's hand pulling her to their doorway. "We'll talk to y'all later." He shut the door firmly behind them. If he tried to be subtle, he failed.

Ryder looked at me and shook his head. I chuckled a little. He followed me to the hallway door and opened it for me. I leaned against the frame before stepping out. "Thanks for making sure I slept in a nice bed last night. I hate that you curled up on the couch."

He glanced back at the white linen seating. "It was fine. I've slept on worse."

"I'm sure you have. I know this hasn't always been an easy life on the road."

He ran his hand through his mussed hair and down the back of his neck. The other hand hooked a thumb in his back pocket. "I enjoyed your company last night. I don't get to do something like that too often."

"No, me either. Thanks for the midnight cheeseburger, too." I looked down the hall. "Guess I'll go clean up in my room now." Before I could take a step, he wrapped his hand around the back of my neck and eased toward me. I knew what was coming but couldn't find a single reason to stop it.

His lips barely touched mine at first. It was more of a slow, soft brush than a kiss. It felt sweet, but then he stepped into my personal space and kissed me like he meant it. I melted against him and took all he offered. A kiss like that hadn't happened in so long, I got caught up in the fervency of it as I wrapped my arm around his waist.

When he pulled back and rested his forehead on mine, I needed to get my breathing under control. "Uh... thank you," my words whispered from my swollen lips. Nothing else came to mind after he'd wiped my brain cells.

"I want to see you again."

"Okay."

"When?"

"Soon."

"Good."

I nodded, and he let me go. I walked, or maybe it was floated, down the hall to the elevator. Looking back at his doorway, he waved before shutting the door. As soon as I stepped into the empty elevator, I sucked in a deep breath trying to restore my depleted oxygen.

"Wow." I didn't know if I'd ever been kissed that thoroughly before. As the car descended to my floor, I thought back over last night. He'd held me in front of the city lights until I slept. I didn't remember walking to the bed.

Surely, he didn't carry me. I'm too heavy for that. My body wasn't like Chandler's. I tried to take care of myself, but I'd been known to binge on chocolate ice cream occasionally. He must have known that after watching me put away my dinner last night.

Working out wasn't my favorite thing to do either, but I did like to run a few days a week so I could fit into my jeans. My curves didn't bother me, though. A

Ryder Steel

grown woman should have curves at forty, even if I never had children. He didn't seem to mind, though, when he asked about seeing me again.

I smiled to myself thinking about his last words as I opened the door to my room. This could be an interesting tour.

I turned on the water of my average shower in an average hotel room. "Maybe one day I'll make the kind of money that affords suites on top floors with oversized spa showers," my voice echoed off the tiles as I stepped under the warmth.

My phone rang as I stepped from the bath area. It was my assistant checking in since I again forgot to do so.

"What's going on, Trudy?"

"Just wanted to see if everything there was under control." I heard her tapping on her keyboard as she spoke.

"Yes, it's all good here. I lined up some ideas on the way here about places I wanted to shoot today. The sun's out, so I'll have some natural light for the ones I wanted to get in Central Park." I pulled my leggings on while talking which was no easy feat. "What about there?"

Thia Finn

"I've done most of today's list already, but you know how that goes. As soon as I think I'm done, someone will call or come in and screw it all up."

"Sorry, but I'm confident you'll take care of everything. I'll be back soon, and we'll go over all that needs to be handled while I'm with the bands."

"Sounds good." I heard her shuffling papers. "Oh, you had an interesting call from a man."

"A man?"

"Yes. He's a band manager and wanted to set up a time for you to meet up and shoot them on stage."

"What's so strange about that?" I had calls like this all the time.

"For one thing, he wouldn't leave his information. Never even said his name, even though I asked more than once."

"That's weird. Did he leave call-back info?"

"No, that's the other thing. He said he would call back because he was calling from a temporary number. Who conducts business from a temporary number?"

"Good question. If he does call back, tell him I'm not interested, too busy, something. Make up an excuse. He's probably a scammer anyway, so we aren't getting involved in that."

Ryder Steel

"Right. I should have said that as soon as he started being evasive."

"Yeah, but you didn't know. I mean, how often do we get those calls?"

"I'm going to say never before, but he knew the business and your name, and that you were in New York with the Steel tour."

"What? How would he know that unless he was at the show and saw me?"

"Who knows? There're crazies everywhere these days. I'll put a stop to it if we hear from him again." I had faith in Trudy. She knew how to handle everything about my business.

"Okay, I'm going to run. Don't want to lose the light or be late to my paying gig."

"Right. Have fun, boss."

"You, too, boss two." We always joked about that. I owned it, but she knew the business end of my company better than I did. I had enough to worry about besides dealing with numbers, which was something I hated.

I heard a knock on the door as I gathered my camera bag. Peeping through the keyhole, I spotted Ryder standing there in his usual thumb-in-pocket stance.

Thia Finn

"Hello," he greeted before the door opened completely. "You ready to leave?" He looked down at my bag in hand.

"Yeah. How'd you time that so perfectly?"

"Didn't. Just took a chance you'd had enough time to get more beautiful."

"Oh, now he's all about cheesy lines." I giggled, something I never did.

"I thought women liked being told they were beautiful."

"You're right. Sorry. Thank you. I guess it sounded strange."

"Strange that I said it, or strange that I think you're a beautiful woman?"

"Hmm... maybe both."

"G'Anna, you are gorgeous. Men haven't been telling you enough if you're unaware of it."

When was the last time I'd been told that by a man? I needed to work on my social life more. I looked up at him and smiled. "Thank you. I mean, for saying that. And no, I don't hear it often since I rarely go out."

"Why not?" I stepped into the hallway, and he pulled the door closed.

As we waited for the elevator, I turned to him. "I guess I don't have time. I've been so busy trying to

Ryder Steel

grow my business that I forget I need a social life, too."

"And none of your customers ask you out? I find that hard to believe."

I came back immediately with an incredulous, "Well, it's true. A couple tried in the beginning but encouraging clients to see me as something other than my job never worked too well for me."

Before the door opened, Ryder pulled a ball cap from his back pocket. I stared as he put it on. It had long hair pulled in the back into a ponytail.

"Really? That's your disguise for the public?" I covered my laughter with my hand.

Next, he donned dark sunglasses. "Sure is. You like it?"

"Uh... I think it might draw more attention."

"No, I'll look like every other New Yorker who works as a photographer's assistant." He reached down and took my two bags of equipment. The backpack he slung over his shoulder. "Okay, I'm ready."

The door opened, and he stepped out. I watched him and thought maybe he was right, but who said he was coming with me?

"What are you doing anyway? I didn't ask you to help."

Page | 121

"No, but if we're going to have any time together and you get your work done, I need to go with you."

"It's going to be a lot of walking." We turned and crossed the street heading to the park.

"Good. I need to get my cardio in, and I missed the gym this morning."

"Something you do daily, I assume?" I knew he looked great under that shirt. His stomach felt rock hard when he held me against him last night as we looked out over the skyline.

"I try to. I'd gotten out of the habit, but while I was away, I took advantage of working out with a trainer every day." His hand touched my back as the next light to cross changed, keeping it there while we moved along with the other pedestrians.

Not thinking about what he said, I asked, "Away?"

He didn't answer right away, but we were in a crowd of people, so I didn't push for one. I stopped at the park entrance near the spot I wanted to take the shots. Reaching for the bag, he put his hand on my wrist keeping me from my task.

"Wait." The look on his face told me he wanted to say something important, so I stood still.

"What is it?"

"Look, I want to tell you the truth, so you don't read shit about me and wonder about it."

"Okay." This sounded serious.

"I have some issues." He took a breath, and I felt the need to validate his words.

"Don't we all?"

"Yeah, maybe, but mine are more serious than some."

I didn't speak this time but nodded my head. He looked around us and then took my hand leading me to a park bench away from listeners.

"If you've read anything about me, you know I have issues with addiction."

"Right. Lots of people do, though, so I didn't make a thing out of it."

"My addiction started from losing someone very special to me, Chandler's mom. I lost them both for a long time when the band was getting started. I told you some of the story at dinner but not everything.

"Chandler's mom left when she was pregnant, and I never knew about her until Chandler contacted me a few months ago. Even before I knew about Chandler, her mom was killed in an accident. Chandler was an infant and had been given up for adoption. I only learned all of this a few months back." My heart dropped.

"It's terrible that you were kept in the dark all these years, Ryder. I'm so sorry. They robbed you of all her growing up." I took his hand and held it in mine to offer him comfort because his face said he still had issues over the loss of her childhood.

"When I found out about Chandler's mom being killed, I lost it. I started a downhill spiral with drugs that really fucked me up. I ended up in rehab for a time, so I could work through the issues. Before overcoming the addiction, I had to deal with the grief of losing my first and only love." He turned and sat back against the bench staring out at the park's sparse wilderness in front of us. I had no intention of pushing him for any more information, so I mimicked his seating.

"When Chandler found me and started telling me the story, I immediately knew who she was. Hell, I knew when I saw her, but facing the truth was too hard. I called my doctor and checked myself into the rehab facility for a few days. Trying to self-medicate again after all those years to deal with the resurfacing feelings could happen too easily." He squeezed my hand as if he were holding on. It made me glad to be there.

"I'm generally a strong person, G'Anna. I can deal with shit from everyone else and for my family and friends, but when this sweet, beautiful, young woman stood in front of me only seeking acknowledgment of her existence, I freaked out. Everything from over twenty years ago rushed back at me like a freight train hell-bent on keeping a schedule. I called the doctor and flew off to Arizona as soon they readied the jet."

The silence filled in around us with children's noises as moms with strollers jogged past. New Yorkers' nannies walked by holding the hands of small children as they made their way to afternoon playdates. Did these sounds resonate with Ryder after the story he shared?

He finally turned to me. "If you don't want to see me anymore, I completely understand. I'm still broken from what they stole from me, and if you don't want any part of that, I get it."

"Why would I think that, Ryder? You've been nothing short of wonderful to me. From the interaction between you and Chandler, I see you're creating a relationship for the two of you which will last forever. Isn't that the most you can hope for? Honestly, you don't owe me an explanation at all. I mean, we've only been out on one date."

"Yes, I know, but I think this could be more, and I wanted you to know what you're getting into up front. I don't want to develop feelings for someone who's going to run at the first sign of trouble, and I guarantee there'll be trouble. If not from my issues, then from fans and the paparazzi. I'm shocked as shit they haven't found me already, and when they figure out we are together, they'll come after you, too. Sometimes, I think they've implanted a tracker on my body that shoots a beacon up showing where I am every single minute."

"I believe everything you've said until that." We both laughed.

"Honestly, G'Anna, I'd like to see where this could go if you're all in. With me and my life, there's no halfway. We deal with the shit along the way and enjoy the privacy we can get. I'm working through the bouts of depression as they come and go, hoping that spending more time with Chandler ends some of them."

I leaned over and kissed his cheek. "I believe I can work with it."

"Good. Now, let's go shoot some pictures. I'm feeling photogenic today." I slapped his chest at his crazy comment. When was he not photogenic?

Chapter 14

RYDER

"Goodnight, Boston." I waved at the audience in our second city and threw my pick into the audience. This would be our last performance before heading overseas in a couple of days. The kids' performances for the three U.S. shows brought them to the spotlight, and we hoped it would increase their fan base even more.

They didn't need us to help out with that. Their music spoke for itself. The fact they had a look all women craved and a sound all fans loved didn't hurt either. The music and lyrics drew the fans in, too. They were written from the heart and told of the old tropes and issues listeners desired.

Walking to the wings, I spotted my favorite photographer talking to my favorite A.D. members.

"The show sounded fucking awesome, Ryder. Hell, we all knew it would." KeeMac patted me on the back. I didn't need his validation, but it made me feel great to know an up-and-coming singer and songwriter appreciated our sound.

"Thanks."

"Yeah, Ryder. Y'alls' fans go crazy for your new stuff as much as your old music," Chandler added. "We can only hope that we develop fans who'll follow us for a lifetime."

I looked up at her. My daughter's beauty mimicked her mother's in every way both inside and out. "Thanks, Chandler. I appreciate hearing that from you youngsters in the business."

KeeMac stuck his chest out. The boy's actions reminded me of all of us when people called us young. He'll get a thrill out of it when he turns forty. "We're not some punk-ass youngsters anymore, Ryder."

"Get your feathers back under control, Leghorn. I only meant that you're younger in comparison to Steel."

"Yeah, that's for damn sure, old man."

I turned in time to see Chandler slap his abdomen. "Don't worry, Dad, I got this under control."

"Is that right? He calls me old again, and he'll see how fast I can drop his ass." I popped him on the back of the head.

"Hey, one hit's enough. I get it." Chandler and I shared a smile.

"I'm thinking you don't since we've been down this road already. I'm not old, and you're not young. I get it." I reached down and grabbed G'Anna's free hand where she stood watching the sparring. "You agree with me, G'Anna?"

"Don't get me between the two of you, but I'll be here to get the money shot when you knock him in the dirt." She snickered at her comment but held up her camera that hung from the neck strap.

"Well, damn. I thought you were here to snap fucking photos of hot musicians to sell to magazines and make those cool millions. I didn't realize you needed abuse to make the money." KeeMac's joking tone kept the conversation light as we made our way to the backstage after party. "Shit, get a good pic of my babe kissing her favorite fucking rock god."

As he turned to finish his statement by lip-locking with her, she stepped forward and kissed Ryder on the cheek leaving the cocky boyfriend bewildered.

"Damn, babe, that's not fair. I meant me."

She turned and grinned at him. "You said my favorite rock god." She swung her attention to me and added, "I did what you asked, so G'Anna could capture a great moment between us. You got it, right?"

G'ANNA

"Sure did, and it looks great in the viewfinder. Want to see?" Chandler moved to my side as we made our way in the door of the full-blown party going on. Both bands' members started the party without us.

Women made their way in the bands' direction the moment the door slammed shut behind us by the bodyguard.

"Sign my concert t-shirt, please."

"I'll show you my tits if you'll sign them."

"Did you catch my double D sequined bra when I threw it at you?"

The comments came from all sides.

I stepped away and focused my camera, listening to some of the absurd questions and comments while shooting the unfazed looks on the two singers' faces. Those photos were priceless in my book. Some women's sincerity brightly glowed while others made my gag reflex jump into full action. They were there for one reason only—sex with the superstars for the bragging rights.

Why did women debase themselves this way? Some would turn and cry foul when the front men used them and sent them on their way, and others would rejoice in their luck of having these men. The former's actions made me feel like they undermined everything most women fought daily in a man's world. I stood looking at them but refused to shoot a single shot that disgusted me.

"Take our picture," a dyed redhead barked as she wrapped her arms around Ryder's neck and rubbed her almost bare body against him. The comical look on his face made the shot worth it, though. I could blur her out later, never wanting to give credibility to her forced affection.

"She will not shoot a single damn picture with you dangling loose body parts on me. If I wanted a Steel Stripper, I'd asked. Go find Joel. I hear he's in the market for a new favorite." Ryder pealed the woman off him being careful not to touch exposed flesh.

Guess no one would see that shot.

As she walked away, I let my camera dangle from the neck strap. KeeMac doubled over laughing, and Chandler's eyes followed the woman across the room. "There are no words for women like that," she finally said loud enough for everyone around us to hear. Clearly, she wanted no part of a Steel Stripper latching onto her lover the way they did Ryder.

"Please tell me you didn't shoot a picture of that scene." Ryder's voice came out low and raspy.

"I did, but no one will ever know it was her. She'll be blurred out."

"If you could lose the photo, I'd be happier. The Strippers know I don't fucking work that way."

His frank comment caused me to hit the delete button. "Gone."

Before we moved on, I found myself wondering how I felt about these women being around at all. I quickly decided the convenience of a warm body waiting and willing irked me. Ryder and I weren't actually a thing, but he'd said he wanted to see where we might be headed, and so did I.

A chance for anything physical to happen between us hadn't occurred yet. I felt like it might have happened somewhat faster, but events and people got in the way. Now I knew if he had a pick for the night, why would he want me in his bed? I doubted I could hold a candle to the skills these women packed in their bags of tricks.

"Thank God. I never want a picture surfacing of me with one of them in that type of pose. We dealt with all of that years ago, but it doesn't stop them from always trying." He reached down and took my hand holding it up between us. "I'm sure she saw this when we walked in, and a jealous streak rushed down her back. Some of them know no limits." He turned and took a step toward the food and beverage tables tugging me along behind him.

We admired the spread of goodies displayed. "I like this catering company. We might need to see if they can do overseas work at some point." My mind still hovered around the knowledge I considered, and I didn't respond. "What's wrong?"

I looked up at him through my lashes, and his head cocked to the side.

"What's going on, G'Anna? Did I say something wrong? Did you see something that bothers you?" He stepped directly in front of me, so I could only see the black of his t-shirt covering the pecs that stretched it.

"Uh... no. Nothing's wrong."

His warm hand cupped my chin tilting it upward until I looked into his probing eyes. "Must be something. We were discussing photos, then food before I lost you to something else." He offered no relief when he continued to look at me with an unwavering view.

Thia Finn

"I don't know. It's stupid." I placed my hands on his chest. Maybe it was to hold on, maybe I needed the contact. I didn't know which.

"Nothing's stupid if you aren't comfortable about something."

"I'm a grown woman and should be secure in myself."

"You exude confidence, sugar," he said this with conviction as though he never doubted me about anything.

I glanced from side to side. Beautiful people held light conversations all around us. Laughter could be heard from every direction. I took pictures of celebrities on a daily basis, so why was I having a hard time? Why was now any different?

Finally, I looked back up at Ryder. His bearded chin, his perfect lips, his kind eyes all held my gaze. "I guess I'm not used to being part of this crowd. I'm usually the person on the fringes doing my thing with a camera. Now, I'm in the middle of it all. It's a little overwhelming."

He pulled me into him. "Don't worry, sugar. I got you."

After that he kept me close the entire party.

In my heart, I knew this was all a huge lie. I was scared shitless. Here I stood with stunning women

P a g e | **134**

staring at the one thing they wanted—Ryder Steel. The question I should have asked him is what did he want?

RYDER

My entourage, minus Chandler and KeeMac, finally made it back to the hotel with bodyguards and a few extra women in tow. Joel didn't disappoint when it came to claiming his perfect woman. I stepped out turning to help a quiet G'Anna. Her silence lasted through the party, and she stayed pinned to my side listening as I made my way around the room visiting with the crowd. These parties were necessary because we had nothing without our fans who won contests and the sponsors who conducted them. We learned long ago to happily endure them.

When the elevator doors shut, I wrapped her in my arms and pulled her flush against me. Sparks of lust shot through me as I ignored the rest of the elevator passengers. Family understood me, and maybe they knew my fierce need to share, the excitement with someone after all this time.

I never considered she might not like the idea of others knowing we were seeing each other. Maybe that's why she shut down tonight. I supposed I should've discussed it before I latched on to her at the party. Knowing all the reporters who stood around drinking our booze like I did, they took pictures on the sly. The two of us might be top billing on their media feeds before they sped off to the next party.

"You okay?" I whispered in her ear and then nuzzled her neck.

A soft noise of pleasure responded before she swallowed. My lips moved back to her ear, and I ran my tongue up the rim from top to bottom before taking the petite lobe between my teeth for a tug to the edge. Her body responded with a shudder that I felt run down the length of her torso pinned against me. Definitely one of her pleasure points. I needed to remember that.

She lifted to my ear, whispering, "People are all around us."

A smile formed on my lips as I continued assaulting her senses with delicate kisses under her ear and down her neck until I reached the curve. Here, I bit and dropped soothing kisses.

"Ding, ding." The chime for our floor sounded causing us to move apart.

"I should go to my room tonight."

"This is your room, sugar. Your stuff's already moved, remember?" I pulled the keycard from my billfold. "We should have gotten you a key of your own, but since we're leaving it the morning, guess you don't need one."

As the door opened, I turned back to her. "Do you not want to stay here?" If she said no, I started preparing the reasons why she should change her mind. I held it open so she could walk in first. She looked at it and then moved through the entrance. *Thank God.*

"What I don't want to do is impose. Chandler said this was your family time, and with me here... I might be in the way." Her face dropped as she finished her comment.

"I promise you this, the two of them will be in their room, doing, uh... well, you know what they'll be doing. We won't see them until morning, and if I hear them, I'll make them get their own room at the next stop." I hoped my lighthearted comment removed her apprehension from staying in our suite. I wanted her here, but maybe she didn't understand the hints I'd dropped all evening. Certainly, she felt it on the ride up.

She turned and pierced me with warmth from those deep brown eyes. "The real question is, do you want me here? I mean, you're not simply trying to be nice to include me in the lavish rooms you share?"

"Lavish rooms, huh?" I stepped into her and pulled her into my arms. "I'd want to share the No-Tell Motel with you right now." I dropped my lips to hers and kissed her hard. Our lips, teeth, and tongues tangled for control. My arms tightened around her, and my hands slid down to her fine-for- squeezing ass.

With a cheek in each hand, I ground her against my growing length and a deep moan worked its way up her throat and into my mouth setting off another round of plumping and grinding. Breaking away from her lips, I bit down on the opposite neck from before. Nips and licks that might have left marks ran from below her ear to her collarbone. Her head lolled back allowing me better access to the tender skin of her throat, and I assaulted it with equal passion back up to her swollen red lips.

Sucking her lower lip into my mouth, I ran my tongue across the soft flesh. Damn, this woman started a fire inside me that wasn't going away anytime soon, until the door swung back hard enough to crash into the wall behind it. We broke apart in time to see Chandler's legs wrapped around the tall body of her lover's as he slammed her into the wall and kicked the door closed. He ground against her, and I felt sure it would have been actual sex if clothes didn't block the way.

"Uh-hmm," I let out. "Go to your fucking room for that, please."

Chandler dropped her legs from his waist, and he stood her on her feet. "Oh, sorry, Ryder. We didn't know you were still awake." If circumstances of our lives had been different, this would have been a great father-daughter moment, one we could laugh at later on in life. Since we were still in an infant stage, my reaction to their lust for each other still bothered me.

"You have a room. We'd appreciate it if you'd use it." Trying not to sound like a total buzzkill for them, I added, "Or we can go to another room if y'all need us to."

"No, not necessary." Chandler took KeeMac's hand and dragged him to their room shutting the door but not before we heard his loud laughter and "busted."

G'Anna looked at me. "Was he talking about them or us?" And she started laughing, too.

Ryder Steel

"Dammit, this whole dad thing can be annoying at times." I smiled at her because we both knew I loved every minute of having my daughter with me.

"Don't suppose you want to make our way into my room and pick up where we left off, do you?" My eyebrow cocked up as I asked.

"You know what? I'm kinda tired, and we do have to get up early in the morning." Knowing my face held disappointment, she added, "Maybe we should save it for another time."

I sucked in a deep breath and let it out. "I guess you're right, but I am going to hold you to 'another time.'" I walked over to the door where her luggage waited inside and opened it. "Goodnight, sugar." I bent and gave her an easy kiss. Fuck, I wanted more.

She slid through the doorway and turned grabbing the side of the door. "Goodnight, Ryder Steel."

I stood looking at the white panel separating me from what I wanted. In another time, I would have kicked that son of a bitch down and taken what I wanted, but now, I'm a different man. Hell, I've been a different man for a long time. Women didn't affect me this way anymore, so what changed when G'Anna walked onto this scene?

Walking to the bedroom that held my empty bed, my head needed to wrap around this situation. Did I

P a g e | **141**

Thia Finn

want her in my bed because it was easy? No, nothing about her would be easy. No, instinct told me the beautiful woman behind the wall came into my life for more than easy. The real question that plagued me now was, am I ready for her?

G'ANNA

The departure date in three days highlighted the saved email I read on my phone as I sat back during take-off. When I snuck out of the suite this morning, I considered waking Ryder to say goodbye, but I knew we'd be seeing each other soon, so I let them all sleep. My flight left early, and I had no idea when they would take off. I should have taken Chandler up on the flights to and from Boston but business called.

Resting my head back, I glanced at the man seated next to me. His even breathing told me he slept through the take-off. Lucky him. I could never do it.

I finished looking at the itinerary for the tour. The band wanted me to travel the entire tour taking pictures, but my busy schedule said otherwise. Trudy would hold down the fort while I enjoyed shooting in several European locations.

I wanted to capture scenery and places I'd never visited before. I hoped there would be time for it. I pulled up my notes app and looked over the places I considered as a must-see. Finding the right moment to escape the bands would be the key.

Would Ryder be interested in coming with me on some of my side trips? I hoped so, but maybe he felt like he needed to be with Chandler to sightsee. They could discover the world together. What better way to get to know each other? Who wouldn't want that with their long-lost parent?

A ding from my phone startled me back to reality, never having gotten used to the idea that messages were now acceptable on flights.

It read, "Call me." I didn't recognize the number attached to it, so I deleted the brief note.

The ding happened again within a few minutes. "Call me, please." I stared at the same number from our area code. Maybe Trudy got a new number for some reason, so I typed out, "In the air. Talk later." No reply came. I decided it must have been her.

As my chair leaned back, I closed my eyes thinking about the past weekend. My time with Ryder rattled my brain first. What a strange weekend it was with him. Hanging around with celebrities in relaxed atmospheres as we'd been in happened all the time. I took the opportunity to shoot picture after picture. Having a photo pass to backstage, I enjoyed taking candid shots. Nothing like this weekend had ever been on my radar. Experiencing the behind-the-scene situations gave me a whole new perspective.

I admitted to myself that some of it I enjoyed, some of it disgusted me, and some of it freaked me out. Rolling with the band might not be a life I could take on a full-time basis. The best part came from the intimacy I shared with Ryder. Remembering the scratches from his beard on my face and neck, I felt the heat running up my face.

That man kissed me senseless more than once. I'd never experienced kisses that caused me to lose all thought. My mind disintegrated with his lips on me. It didn't matter if my lips, ear, or neck were the recipient of those little nips he took from my skin. My ability to think sprouted wings when the warmth from his tongue wielded licks against the sensitive spots on my neck.

I'd had more than one long-term relationship in my years. This would probably not be one, though. As the tour ran its course, so would our chance at a relationship. His life consisted of wherever the band took him. My life followed a pattern—shooting, editing, selling.

Most of my band work happened in Austin. People referred to it as the live music capital of the South. Flying off to venues all over the world wasn't necessary when I could catch so many of the greatest bands in my hometown. I knew enough about every venue that choosing spots to shoot from became second nature to me.

Steel played most of the venues over the twenty plus years they'd been together. Even though lots of them had changed names over the years, little else had changed. Living in the city also helped me meet the owners and managers which gave me an advantage in most cases. They allowed me backstage, entrance without a ticket, and access to the holding rooms.

The difference between Ryder and me was he traveled constantly, and I usually stayed in one place. Since Ryder shared their story with me, I understood why they needed to have this time allowed to them during the tour. Chandler truly wanted me to record their reuniting, so I agreed to travel with them. After the weekend I now flew home from, the tour took on a whole new perspective.

I woke to the plane preparing to land, and the flight attendant tapping me on the shoulder. "Sorry to wake you, but you were sleeping pretty hard, and you need to bring your seat back up." I punched the button and looked out the uncovered window in my row surprised I'd slept that long. My fingers ran around my mouth to make sure drool hadn't dripped down my chin.

After disembarking, I collected my bags and car, I took off for the studio. Trudy's text said there were things I needed to deal with so I bypassed going home. When I looked at my phone, that same number had left one that I didn't bother to look up. I needed to block that number, so no more landed in my inbox.

The quiet of the studio scared me since it was usually nonstop controlled chaos. Trudy sat behind her desk with paperwork piled all over it. She looked up as I stepped in front of it. "Oh, hey. Didn't hear the door open."

"Let's get a bell or something for the door. You need to know when someone comes in. I never realized you didn't hear it." I wanted to rant about this because of the safety but held off for now.

"I don't know if I could stand that noise all day."

"Not that many people come and go, but I'd like you to know when they do."

"Thanks, boss. I appreciate you looking out for me after all this time." She gave me a little smirk.

"What's going on to have you so focused on one thing?"

"Trying to get all of your details lined out for the trip. I know you like a clean schedule to work from."

"Yeah, that'd be great. I hope the band doesn't have other ideas. You know I like to be flexible to work around them."

"Right. I talked to the people over at 13 Recordings this morning to get any last-minute changes."

One reason I loved this girl, she always took care of the little details. "Great. Thanks for handling all of that. I hope there's not too many."

"No, very few actually which surprised me. I guess when you're dealing with a mega-band like Steel, plans are pretty much etched in stone. Can't have any snafus with thousands of tickets sold."

"That's true. All of the venues will be sold out if they aren't already."

"Yeah, I looked online, and most are, so tons of fans will make it interesting for trying to get some of the types of photos I know you like to do. Price of playing huge venues."

I headed to my office as I spoke. "The best thing about them, though, is the large stage they can work with for setting up special effects and various levels. Gives me new perspectives to work with."

My phone rang from the number I needed to block. "Hello. Who is this?"

"Nice way to greet me, sugar." The soft drawl coming over the speaker made my lady bits stand up and take notice. Damn, I needed to get laid if all it took was hearing his voice.

"Oh, hello. I didn't know it was you." I sank into my comfy leather desk chair with a smile on my face.

"I tried catching you before you left. Why didn't you wake me?"

I felt my stomach drop from the guilt. "I knew you needed some restful sleep with the tour about to launch. It's going to be a long four months for the band."

"We're used to it. I wish you'd have let me kiss you goodbye, but you're right, it was probably for the best."

"Oh?" His comment surprised me. Did he not want me hanging around?

"Yeah, if you'd have come into my dark bedroom and started kissing me, I'd probably have pulled you in and rolled until you were under me. All sorts of dirty things come to mind when I consider what I want to do to your luscious body."

"Uh... oh, okay." Did I mention my lady bits had already stood up and taken notice? Yeah, now they shifted to high alert. "Well... I guess I'm sorry I didn't stop then."

"Great answer, sugar. Sounds like we're on the same page." He chuckled. "It's going to happen so be prepared."

I swallowed hard as I considered his idea of dirty things. Damn, I needed to visit with BOB.

RYDER

Our band of misfits, young and old, almost filled the jet. How did my life evolve to this? All we wanted to do was play music, and now we had a whole new generation of musicians traveling with us.

"Hey, Ryder," Chandler called as she and KeeMac made their way toward me. Looking at my beautiful daughter, a sense of pride welled up deep inside me. I had no right to feel this way. She'd had to work so hard to get to me. She'd lived an easy life, but for some reason, it seemed like her childhood lacked in some ways.

Thinking about all I'd missed sent fountains of guilt pouring over me. I should have been more diligent in finding her mother. I should have been a better boyfriend and never allowed Lainey to drive home alone that night. I should have been sitting beside her when she saw the test results. God, I hated myself for letting the years slip through my fingers.

"Ryder..." she put her hand on mine, "... what's wrong?"

"It's nothing, baby girl." I took her small hand in mine wondering how it felt holding it when she was truly a baby girl.

She leaned over to speak softly, "You look so sad like you've lost your best friend."

Kissing the back of her hand, I murmured, "When you're with me, I'm never sad." I tried deflecting her comments, but she saw right through my attempts.

"You know you can tell me anything. I feel like we've been through hell already, so everything else has to be heaven, right?"

How did I get this lucky? "Little girl, I love the woman you've become. My only wish is I could take some credit for it."

She met my face with a soft smile. "The good thing is we have the rest of our lives to mold each other into a great family, and that's going to be so much longer than the first twenty-one years."

I nodded at her. Luckiest fucker alive.

The jet settled out at thirty thousand feet when the attendant came out with beverages. They never offered me alcohol, but the others drank around me. It used to bother me, but now it feels like another lifetime ago. Nothing about drinking appealed to me anymore.

"Hey, I thought that pretty little photographer would be on the ride over with us," Joel called from across the aisle.

"Thought so, too, but she had other plans for today. Had to get back sooner than we all wanted to roll out." I closed my eyes and tried to sleep, but Chandler came aboard with other plans for me.

"Ryder?" I barely heard her whisper.

"Yes?" I said without opening my eyes.

"I wanted to talk to you about G'Anna."

"Is that right? What about her?"

"You know it's okay to have a girlfriend."

This caused me to grin still having my eyes closed. "A girlfriend at my age is kinda funny."

"No, it's not. Why should you be alone?" She wasn't going to let this go either. Chandler reminded me of a bulldog I once had, only a lot prettier.

"I'm a grown man, Chandler. I'll decide if I need a girlfriend."

Thia Finn

"I just thought when I saw G'Anna in our suite, that maybe, you know..." she trailed off.

"I know, huh?"

KeeMac chimed in. "She's trying to tell you that it's okay to sleep with women in your own damn room."

"Is that right? Well, I guess I'd have never figured that out." I shook my head. His bluntness never ceased to amaze me.

"Hell yeah. Chan's afraid you're lonely even with all of us around. If our being in your room is stopping you, we'll move to our own room." Chandler swung her head around and mouthed something at him. He leaned back and closed his eyes.

I snickered to myself. "Look, baby girl, if I want a female in my room, I'll take care of it. You worry about keeping the big guy beside you happy."

"He is happy. Look at him." KeeMac's genuine smile told me they were good. "We want you to be happy, too."

"What are you getting at Chandler?"

"G'Anna is a great woman. She's easy to get along with, and I happen to know she's not currently involved with anyone."

"Oh yeah. That's good to know." I peeled one eye open and looked at her. "So, no one waiting back in Austin for her?"

Page | **154**

"No, I've never seen her with a guy or even talk about one. I'm guessing it's been a while, so she's definitely on the market."

"Baby girl, she is not a piece of meat. Please don't say things like that about her. We've spent some time together this weekend, and I enjoyed every minute of it. We'll see where it goes, but don't worry about me I can take care of my own love life."

"The thing is... I don't want you to feel like it's going to make things weird for us. I'm not a little kid who has to approve of the person you see or is going to be angry that you're trying to take my mother's place."

I turned and looked at her. I'd never considered this for one minute. "Has this been bothering you?"

She nodded her head. "I wasn't trying to pry or anything but... I might have asked the other members of Steel about the women you've been seeing." She held up her hands when my eyebrows shot to my hairline. "Wait. Don't get all mad. I simply asked if you had a girlfriend and if you'd had many over the years."

"Why would you ask them that? Why in the hell didn't you ask me? I'll always tell you the truth, Chandler."

"I know, but I didn't know if you'd get angry talking about other women in your life."

Thia Finn

"Let me tell you this, baby girl. There is nothing you can't ask me. I'm here for you until the day I die. I meant what I said earlier." She obviously needed more assurance about me.

"So, did I. That's why I wanted to talk to you about women."

"What you're saying is all of this conversation started, so you could ask me about G'Anna?" She nodded her head. "G'Anna and I are good, Chandler. I spoke to her this morning before I got out of bed. I told the truth about her leaving. She had some work to do in her office so she can leave on the tour. That's the reason she left early, and she's already back there now." The longer I spoke, the bigger Chandler's smile got. "Are we good on this subject now?"

"Yes, we're good." She threw her arms around me and hugged me tightly. "We're perfect." I pulled her to me. Getting a hug from your daughter couldn't be any sweeter.

Large SUVs waited on the tarmac close to the hangar as we disembarked the jet. The band went their separate ways as everyone was ready to spend time around Austin before the long trip across to Europe. We parked in the parking garage of the hotel where I currently called home.

As KeeMac stepped out from the back seat and Chandler followed, he said, "I think we're going to head back to my house to get things arranged to leave."

"I thought you two were going to stay with me here." I didn't want to go back to spending my time alone.

Chandler spoke up, "We are, but we need to go start gathering all the things we need for the trip. We'll be back later this evening before dinner."

"Oh, right. I'm sure y'all have a lot to do to get ready for being gone for four months." I waved to them as the car backed out of the lot. The bellman had taken my luggage, so I caught the elevator.

The walk into my suite felt empty and lonely. This triggered my depression. I'd learned to deal with my problems a long time ago. Staying busy was key, so I pulled my phone out and texted G'Anna.

Ryder: *Busy*
G'Anna: *Not terribly. Put out a few fires*
Ryder: *Any burn you :)*
G'Anna: *No, thank God*
Ryder: *Plans*
G'Anna: *No, but I'm thinking about a nap. The flight was too early*

Ryder: *Come over and sleep here. My room is empty*

G'Anna: *Hadn't been home yet. Come to my house*

Ryder: *Talked me into it. Address?*

I rummaged around in the closet and pulled out the two helmets for my Harley and my leather jacket. It had been forever since I'd ridden it, but it traveled with the roadies, so I always had it. Riding my girl always made me feel free especially around the Austin area. I knew great places to ride for miles without traffic once you got outside the city.

She started up with the sweet rumble—music to my ears. I took shipment on the custom *Harley* about five years after we made it big. A ride settled my nerves when I had her beneath me. Convincing G'Anna to ride the bike with me might take some doing, but how could she say no to this beauty?

I pulled up to her home in an area west of downtown. Cute little house that looked like something she'd choose. I shut the bike down and walked to the door. It popped open before I could hit the first knock.

"Oh, wow. I heard that sound and knew it had to be you." Her beauty caused an instant balm to my loneliness.

Ryder Steel

I turned and looked at the bike. "Yeah, not something you'd want to use to sneak up on someone."

"Come in. I walked in maybe five minutes ago myself." She turned and headed back into the house. "Want something to drink?"

When I walked in the kitchen area, an excellent sight greeted me. A perfect peach stuck up as she dug around in the refrigerator. "I have some diet drinks, tea, wine, sparkling water. Anything sound good?"

She peeked over her shoulder and busted me staring. She grinned at me and stood up quickly. "Guess that was an interesting view, huh?"

"Better than interesting, in my book." I stepped forward and pulled her into my arms pressing my lips to hers. I heard the fridge door shut before I pushed her into the smooth stainless steel. I licked across the seam of her lips, and she opened allowing me access to her soft tongue.

Her hand looped around the back of my neck as she leaned her head to allow us both better access to deepen the kiss. As we dueled for space, I couldn't help pressing harder into her, grinding against her. I felt a slight hint of hipbones against my lower abs. Her body fitted to mine ideally with her curves submitting against my sharp angles when I pushed against them.

I felt like a teenager when my dick stirred to life with the easy contact. Damn, this wasn't going to be simple to control. Maybe I didn't want to control my pleasure with G'Anna. She would shut it down if I came on too strong too quickly.

The kiss broke, but I continued down from the corner of her mouth, across her smooth cheek to her jaw leaving soft kisses. I didn't want this moment end, and I needed her to know I wanted her.

G'ANNA

Damn, damn, damn, this man. Was he trying to kill me? Every time we were alone, he broke through the thin wall I kept up against men. First, he kissed me like it was the last one left on earth, and now he was nipping at my neck. My resistance ran so shallow at this point. This needed to move to the next level.

He backed away enough to continue the kisses and nips down my neck. Letting go of my ass with one hand, it crept up my side until it covered my breast with a simple squeeze. My nipples stood at attention from the kiss, so when he captured it between his thumb and index finger, a moan escaped from deep in my throat.

My hands raced to my shirt, and I pulled the buttons through the holes just short of ripping it open. I needed his hands on my skin. He got the message loud and clear because he reached up and unclasped my bra from behind me allowing my somewhat sagging boobs to escape. At that moment, I didn't care.

The kisses continued down as he pulled my shirt over my shoulders letting it hit the kitchen floor. My bra followed. He leaned back and looked at my face as he palmed each one. Again, the light squeeze to them happened, but he lifted their weight up as he dropped his eyes to them.

A barely audible "Perfect" escaped before he licked around the pebbled nipple and then sucked it in his warm mouth tonguing the peak while he tortured the other with his thumb and finger. The harder the suction, the more he tweaked the other sending shooting tendrils of desire straight to my throbbing core and had me writhing against him. I wanted this more than anything I desired in a long time.

I pulled his hand off me and took it in mine causing him to remove his mouth. "We need to move this to the bedroom. Now. Please."

With a sweltering look, he nodded. No more words were needed. We'd fought this long enough in New

York and Boston. The hardness I'd felt against me said he felt the same way.

The heat from his body told me he stayed close to me as I dragged him to my bedroom. I kicked off my shoes at the door and started on my jeans.

"G'Anna, stop," he called just inside the doorway.

No way. He couldn't stop now. He revved up my senses against my refrigerator. Surely, he didn't want to back out. "W-What?" I turned to face him.

"Slow down. We're not in a race here. I want you. No, it's more than that, sugar. I need you. I plan to take you, but I'm not rushing through it. We've danced around this moment for the entire weekend. We both need to savor every single moment, so take a beat and let me love you right."

Love me? This isn't about love. This is about fucking, plain and simple. The look on my face must have said everything I thought because he stepped close and wrapped me in his arms.

"Sugar, I'm going to make love to you all night if you let me, and we'll do it any way you want."

Okay, I could get on board with that. I looked up into his gorgeous face. "I think I can let you do that. All night, you say?"

"All fucking night." He lips came down on mine, and by the time he pulled back, he was lying on top of me with my legs wrapped around his waist. He started the descent down my neck all over again, and when he got to my breasts, he stopped to pay homage to each one. I couldn't help but push back against the grinding he did, hitting a spot that screamed needy. God, it felt like heaven having him on top of me, licking and kissing and biting my skin.

As he bit and soothed spots I knew would leave little marks on my skin, my desire for him ramped to new heights. What was this man doing to me? Sex with other men had been good but compared to this, they were like two teens groping in the backseat of a car.

He reached my belly button and kissed around it while hooking his fingers in my unbuttoned jeans. Thank goodness for spandex because when he started pulling, they slid over my hips where he included my panties in the tug. He stood and pulled them off leaving me naked before him.

My usual self-consciousness went out the window with Ryder. He took me in from top to toes, lifting them where he kissed the arch of each foot before spreading my legs enough to get his head between them. He dropped kisses up both legs as his beard softly grazed my skin. The feeling was both soothing and excruciating. I wanted him badly.

I must have let out a moan as he reached my knee because he stopped and looked at me.

"You okay?"

"I'm more than okay. You're driving me crazy." I grabbed the material of my comforter and bunched it up in my fists.

"Good. You'll remember this moment for a long time. How I slowly ambushed every single inch of your body with my mouth so it begged for the spot coming next. I want your body to know my feel, my touch, my bite on every soft spot." He kissed the inside of my other knee before he knelt on the bed and spread my legs wider.

I stopped long enough to look at my opened apex. "Your pussy is perfect, too. Pink and glistening with your desire for me. That's just what I want, G'Anna. I want you to need me so badly by the time I slide into you, you'll scream my name loud enough to wake the neighbors."

Didn't he know I was already there? The full alert he had my senses on should have been sending out smoke alarm sirens to the masses. All I could do was stare at him as he dropped soft kisses up my thighs while I hung onto the material for dear life.

He stopped at the crease between my leg and body and sat up on his knees to pull his t-shirt off. The sheen on his skin helped define every delicious cut between his pecs and each toned abdominal muscle. What he did to me affected him, too, which made me needier.

His hands wrapped around my inner thighs at my knees, and he slid up the skin pushing my legs further apart. He laid down so his mouth was where I needed it to be. When his nose touched my skin, and he ran it up my slit breathing in my essence waiting for him. I wanted to scream.

"Your scent tells me how much your body is preparing for me, sugar. I fucking love it. Now, every time a slight hint of it is around me, I'll know you're waiting for me to take you."

"You're killing me, Ryder. Please." I took his hair in my hand and tried to push him closer to where I needed him.

He gave a little laugh before running his tongue from my entry to my clit causing me to arch up off the bed.

"Holy shit."

"Hmm… guess you like that." He did it again only this time sinking his tongue in further, and when it hit my clit, the moan I cried out might make the police come banging on the door. Too bad because nothing short of death would stop this from happening.

His tongue and fingers worked me over sending my desire soaring. When the two fingers setting me off inside curved upward and rubbed across the roughed skin of my spot, my pleasure burst wide open. I called out to him over and over.

Ryder finally stood and removed his jeans retrieving a condom from his pocket. His hands ran up the length of my body until he reached my neck. I opened my eyes when he gave it a slight squeeze with one palm. "You still with me, G'Anna?"

I smiled. "Oh... hell yeah, I am."

"Good because we're just getting to the best part." After sheathing himself, he leaned down and assaulted my lips. I tasted myself on him. I'd had lovers go down on me before but nothing like what he did to me. Knowing we shared my flavor sent another round of lust down me. This man knew what he was doing.

He pushed up on his forearms and reached between us to slide his rock-hard cock up and down me coating his length. I hadn't had sex in a while, so it made me happy to have something to help him ease inside me.

The head of his thickness stopped at my opening, and he pushed in enough to get the head inside me. "I want to slam into you until I bottom out so badly,

Thia Finn

sugar, but you're tight, and I would never want to hurt you. You know it'll get easier, though."

He pulled out and pushed in again over and over until he was seated all the way. The girth of him stretched me, but I would never complain. The pleasure of his movements had me raising up to meet him with each plunge. Damn, this felt good.

RYDER

Holy shit. Like a damn teenager, I almost blew my load when she came all over my tongue. The pleasure sounds she made, the way my name rolled off her tongue, and her thigh muscles tightening around my ribs, I knew if I took her foot in my hands, her toes had to be curled up. I'd not had a response like that in such a long time, I'd forgotten it existed.

"Sugar, I'm through taking it easy. You good?"

"Oh yeah, I'm so good, I might be dead."

Her response caused a smile on my face. I kissed her again as I began to move harder and faster. She fit me like a glove and dammit if it didn't feel so fucking good, I struggled to breathe.

"Your pussy was made for me, sugar. I love the way it wraps around my cock, and the muscles clamp like it's trying to keep it."

"It is, Ryder. It is." Her breathing was shallow and labored. "It's not going to take much of this to make me come again."

"Good. Come all over my dick." Oh, fuck. What did I ask for? If she came with the force she did with my tongue, I'd follow her right over the edge. I didn't want this to be over that fast. With the pleasure I'd forgotten, we had all night. "I want to feel this pussy clenching down and riding me hard."

"You plan to put me to bed wet?" She knew how the saying went.

"Hell no. I plan to use up every bit of your sweet juices you have to offer." With that, I slammed into her.

"Fuck, yes," she screamed out. I pumped into her over and over as hard as I could, and she took it all. When I pulled one leg up over my arm, she stretched open, and I moved in further. "Oh, Ryder. Don't stop. Don't you dare fucking stop." It seemed like my woman had a dirty mouth like I did during sex. I loved it.

I did stop after a few minutes, though, long enough to step off the bed and stand up, pulling her to the side. With a high bed, her sweet spot met my throbbing dick at the perfect height. Her legs wrapped over my shoulders as my arms came around her thighs spreading her as I pushed back inside her.

This vantage point gave me all I needed to pound into her further and harder which she loved.

"Oh, fucking yes, Ryder. That's perfect. Keep going."

And I did until she screamed my name, or it might have been God's name, or it might have been both of us. All I knew was this was the best fuck I'd had in forever. Her pussy seized me in a fucking chokehold as she came dragging me over the edge to ecstasy.

Her legs had nothing left in them, so I pulled them down to my sides as I crawled over her softness and took her lips in delicate kisses until we could both breathe again. I stayed on my forearms above her knowing we both needed room to expand our lungs.

"Sugar. If it was as good for you as it was for me, I'm surprised we both didn't burn to pieces from the sheer pleasure," I softly whispered in her ear before I rolled off her to my back. "Damn, I might be too old for much of that."

She took in a deep breath and let it out slowly. Her head turned to me, and I met the darkened brown eyes. "Ryder, can we rest and do it again?"

I laughed out loud. "You'll kill me, and I'll die a happy man, but hell yeah."

"Good, we can die together, but right now, I'm exhausted."

"Let me take care of this, and I'll cover us up for a short nap." Soft carpet met my feet as I stood and made my way to her bathroom to dispose of the condom. I wouldn't doubt if the damn latex hadn't broken with all the activity but nothing leaked.

I walked back in the room where she laid on her pillow, her mass of hair covering the pillow. "I hope you're on the pill because I'm going to want to do it without a fucking rubber between us sometime soon." As I climbed into a soft snore, my words went unheard. I spooned her naked body close to me, spreading my hand over her soft stomach. She sighed an easy moan before I closed my eyes.

I woke to a sound I didn't recognize. The warmth from her body ran down my side as her arm draped across my middle and her leg tangled with mine. The noise happened again, and I realized she had to be hungry if the sounds were any indication. I heard her snicker.

She whispered, "Are you awake?"

"Yeah, who could sleep when the hot woman lying all over you has a stomach screaming at them?" I looked down and kissed her pink-tinged face. "We need to feed you."

"I didn't get a chance to eat anything with the flight so early. Sorry."

"Don't be sorry. I'm hungry, too. Want to go out and get something or have something delivered?"

"Do we have to put clothes on to go out?" Her delicious body stretched beside me after she rolled onto her back with her arms thrown above her head. What a sight to wake to. A real woman with curves and natural breasts working out the kinks after the sex we'd shared.

"Hmmm. Yeah, I believe the police might get involved if we don't. I'm not a fan of being naked and arrested." She laughed at my joking attempt.

"No, me neither. Never know who you'll get stuck with, in a cell."

"I've been in a cell a time or two. Nothing about it screams 'this would be better naked.'"

She raised up. "You've been in jail? For what?"

Thia Finn

"Oh, you know. Drunk and disorderly conduct. Public intoxication. That kind of petty shit. We were small time and didn't have a manager or publicist to get us out of it. No worries, though. Money and community service solves a lot of problems."

I stood, walking around the room to find the jeans I'd dropped somewhere. "What's your loud tummy hungry for?" When I looked up at her and saw the way she looked at my dick, I wanted to say, hell yeah and let her have her way with me. "Sugar, you keep checking out my dick, and it's going to rise to the occasion, so you need to either stop or get busy."

Her stomach made a loud noise, and she laughed. "We need to put that on a brief hold and let me eat first. I think I'm going to need some nourishment if your promise from earlier is true."

Oh, I remembered all right. We'd fuck all night long, so I nodded at her and held out my hand.

Room service at home sounded good but was out of the question. I knew places delivered everything these days but getting out and facing the world was important. My security guy waited in the SUV since I'd texted them after I shoved my legs into my jeans and we made our way out to the parking garage. It made me happy G'Anna knew how my life worked.

"They go everywhere we go, right?" she asked when she stepped out and saw the dark vehicle.

"Yeah. Afraid so. I'd rather be afraid of them around than fans or the paparazzi mobbing us. Those people know how to ruin a good time with one click. You're not worried about being seen with me, are you?"

"Why would I be? That's a crazy question, Ryder." From the look she gave me, I knew she believed it.

"Not everyone understands. I figured you would being on the other side of that camera like you are." The door stood open, and she climbed into the back seat.

"Yeah, but I'd never sell my photos to a rag for the sheer purpose of exposing someone's private life." I slid in next to her and wrapped my arm around her dragging her into me. "I know you wouldn't." I turned her to look directly into her eyes. "I trust you, G'Anna. That's not something I say to many people."

She scrutinized my face for sincerity as a few seconds passed. After a visible swallow, she spoke, "I trust you, too, Ryder. I've learned the hard way to only give it to those who truly deserve it. You're one of those people."

After a single nod, my lips met hers in a light telling kiss. We sealed a deal that day.

Chapter 20

G'ANNA

Ryder donned his favorite baseball cap with the long hair sticking out before we stepped from the vehicle. Every time he wore it, I wanted to cackle, loudly. I knew he wore long hair earlier in his life because I'd seen band photos, but the older he grew, the shorter he cut it.

I loved the salt and pepper waves thickly covering the top of his head. A portfolio I'd found of his years in the music business ran in *Rolling Rocks Magazine* a few years back. I owned hard copies of magazines with photos that caught my attention. Steel's spread captured more than my attention. Those guys aged with beauty over their twenty plus years in the business, but Ryder's looks always stood out for me.

His hair had more gray than black now, but it only added to his appeal. From their huge number of fans, their aging hadn't stopped people from loving and admiring them—me being one of the masses.

Billie's on Burnet held only a few patrons when we entered. Ryder let out a breath of relief. I got the feeling he'd like to ditch the band hype at every turn and be a normal person. For beer and burgers, this place was a best-kept secret. He got a Hoss burger, and I tried the Cobra burger, no snake allowed. They arrived, and we both laughed. One would last me a few days. We both managed to put a huge dent in the juicy burgers before we topped them off with interesting named IPAs as we talked of nothing important.

"Dessert? I saw a few on the menu?" I looked up at him.

The smolder he hit me with would've knocked me over if I hadn't been sitting down. "I think we have dessert covered." His hooded eyes trained on me as I blinked, looked down, and gazed to the side. Each time I moved them, I came back to his unmoved ones. Had he even blinked?

"Oookkkaaayyy," I drew the word out knowing what had him ready to throw down money and head out without looking back.

"You ready?"

I nodded at him. He pulled out more than enough cash and dropped it on the table. "That'll cover it. Let's go."

Our ride waited at the curb. Did he stay there the entire time? I turned to Ryder. "Do the two of you have a radar system between you? He's always waiting when we need him."

"Told him to stay here. We wouldn't be long."

"You did, huh? What if I wanted a sweet dessert? You know like *Amy's Ice Cream* or *Tiny Pies*?" I wrapped my hand around his thick bicep.

"We'll have them delivered. I'll feed it to you in bed." His tone was low and gruff.

"Ryder Steel, we can't stay in bed forever." Trying my best to sound resistant to the idea failed.

"No, but I promised you all night long, and it's barely past dark. I don't break promises, sugar." We sat in the darkened car and made out like teenagers fumbling in the back seat on a lost dusty road. When it came to a stop, he opened the door and spoke to our driver, "You can go home for the night. We're not going anywhere until morning."

I started to protest but knew he spoke the truth, so I shut my mouth and climbed out into his arms. He carried me to the door. I unlocked it, and he kicked it shut after flipping the lock back on. "Can't be too careful."

"Who wants you to be careful?" I whispered in his ear.

His phone rang from the pocket of his jeans where he dropped them when we arrived home. Needless to say, he didn't wait to get to the bedroom before he started his delicious assault on me.

The obnoxious noise kept ringing over and over.

"How can you stand that sound?"

He made his way out from under the covers and my arm and leg. "If it's not obnoxious, I usually don't answer it. That's one of the band calling." Sauntering off sans clothing to my den, I heard him rustling around in his jeans.

"What?" Whoa, nice greeting. Not a morning person, if his tone was an indicator. "No, I'm not home. Why are you there?"

I'd heard enough and decided to hop in the shower. After the night we'd spent, I needed more sleep, but a hot shower sounded perfect. Easing some unused muscles that ached was even better.

The warmth flowed down my body bringing back all the positions he'd taken me during the night. The feelings he pulled from me, with his tender words and passionate touches, rushed my mind and caused my face to heat up. I'd never been so thoroughly loved in one night, but there would never be a complaint from me. It had to be the best night of my life. He left me feeling cherished and loved in every sore muscle.

"Dammit. I have to go." He looked around on the floor for his t-shirt.

"Why? It's so early." I stepped from the shower and wrapped a fluffy silver towel around me.

He looked up, and his eyes dropped to it with a smile. "G'Anna, I've seen every exquisite inch of your delicate skin. Covering yourself from me is useless. I like seeing you standing there naked while water inches its way down your body. Reminds me of the best moments of last night when I licked and kissed your liquids from you."

"Ryder," I practically yelled it. "What a thing to say as you are walking out my door." I stepped into him.

He laughed, his arms circling me. "Why? Make you want me to do it again?"

Ryder Steel

"Yeah, it does. Or maybe I could lick you instead. See if it drives you as insane as it does me."

"You talk to me like that, and I'll call the bastards up and tell them to fuck off, I'm busy."

I cocked my eyebrow up trying to entice him, but his phone dinged. "Get your shirt, Mr. Musician. They're waiting for you." He stepped back and took my hand pulling me to my front door. His lips found mine in a heated kiss before he threw the lock.

"Where are you headed anyway? It's kinda early for your band." I realized after I asked it was none of my business. He didn't volunteer the information, and I shouldn't have asked.

"That was Brent. For some reason, all our equipment didn't make the trip back from NYC. People are trying to track it down now. We had hoped to get in the studio at least one day before we left, but we like our own equipment." He hugged me close and kissed my forehead. "I'll call you later and let you know what's going on."

"No problem. I've got to get into the office today. There's more than enough work to keep me busy until the moment the jet leaves." I stepped back, and he leaned in kissing my lips once more. "Go, boss man. They need you."

Page | 181

"Yeah, yeah. That's what Brent said, too." He smiled and picked up his helmet by the doorway. "One day you're going to ride with me."

"Right. We'll see."

Riding on a motorcycle didn't thrill me. It made me nervous thinking about it. I'd seen too many wrecks around this city. The way some of the college kids rode scared me speechless.

I heard nothing when I opened the door to my offices and the studio area which suited me fine. Pictures taken in New York and Boston sat idle on my camera waiting to be culled, cropped, and edited.

With the data card inserted, the red light came on indicating the photos uploading to my hard drive. Several cards waited in line for their turn to present the treasured goodies awaiting. As each card emptied its contents, my anticipation grew. I knew there were some perfect shots in the hordes.

My cell dinged with a message.

Ryder: *Hey, gonna be a while. Equipment found, arriving soon. Running through some new songs and maybe lay down tracks. I'll call later*
G'Anna: *Great on the stuff. I'll be at studio*

Sitting back in my desk chair, I stared at his message. He didn't owe me an explanation, but my heart did a double beat over the fact he gave me one. With a deep breath, I thought about how quickly this thing between us had moved. Was this moving into a relationship? His client status said a bad idea, but damn, the guy was wonderful, kind, and attentive in all the right ways. I crossed my arms over myself. What would happen when this thing between us ran out of steam? We'd be stuck together on the tour, and everyone around us would sense the tension.

I could cut my time short and fly home. Nothing in the contract listed me being there for every single concert. As long as I shot pictures that were noteworthy, there shouldn't be any complaints from the legal people. 13 Recordings wrote iron-clad contracts to protect their interests, but my attorney didn't have any complaints with it.

"Stop it." My words bounced off the walls covered in prints of bands and models. "Stop thinking negative thoughts about what's happening between us."

Talking out loud helped me visualize what my mind created. "Positive thoughts only, G'Anna." I sucked in a deep breath and let the negativity flow out.

As the red light stopped on the drive, an array of beauty filled my screen. Assured Distraction pictures of those hot young guys and Chandler overwhelmed my senses. So much to choose from. It would be difficult to cull any of them.

Starting with the unfocused pictures, I eliminated the obvious. Now for the real work that would take hours to do. My photographer's eyes began the exciting but tedious job.

RYDER

"... the hurt in your eyes." With the last words of the new song sung into the recording mic, I removed the headphones and looked through the control room window at the others who listened. Over the years, that equipment changed so often. We all gave up learning to record music because of it. Besides, we hired the best for that stuff now.

"Sound any good?"

Brett hit a button. "Sounded fucking perfect that time." He wouldn't be the judge, though. The band knew the sound we wanted, and he might be right. I needed to hear it from Dave. His skills made us stars. Some people were born to sing or to play guitar or drums. This guy's talent of getting the perfect sound caused us to go from good to perfect.

Dave listened to the playback through headphones while we waited. His head bobbed slightly to my words. When he pulled them off his ears, he smiled and held up a thumb.

"All right," I spoke into the mic and stepped out of the live room. The rest of the band met me in the hallway.

"Dude, your voice sounded awesome." Poor Joel still hadn't ditched all his Val-speak after all these years.

I laughed. "Right, Joel. Thanks, guys. Is it going to be our next hit?"

"Damn right it is. You owned that bitch." Jason patted me on the back.

"Great. Fucking celebrations in order?"

"Hell yeah, they are. We only came in to practice, but it came together so fast. Let's hit one of our old haunts," Jason continued.

Daniel, the quietest of the band, spoke up, "Man, I feel like playing. Let's go somewhere and do a short set."

"That's a fucking fantastic idea. Continental Club? We've got an open invitation there. Whoever's playing will think it's dope for us to barge in on them," Joel offered.

I shook my head and laughed. "Works for me." We only loaded our guitars knowing a kit and a keyboard would probably be there.

The band hadn't played an impromptu set in ages. With always being on tour, we rarely had time to sit back and simply play for the pure joy of the music. The recording studio sat only a few blocks away, so we loaded into the SUV and headed over.

"All ready to go," Joel told us after looking at his phone. "The manager, John, replied, 'Holy Shit. Steel in our house? I'll kick these dudes off the stage to let you play, even if it's one song.'"

"No!" we all said in unison.

I spoke first, "Tell that dickwad we said not to do that shit. We'd never want to keep a young band from their chance."

"Right, already did," Joel continued. "He's going to cut them short a couple of songs and the later band a few songs, and we'll play in between which is about ten minutes from now."

"Perfect fucking timing. What songs y'all feel like playing?" Brett looked around as he asked.

"We should try the new one out on the crowd. See what kind of response we get from it," Jason suggested.

"Right. Each of you choose one, and mine will be the new one. I'll go third so it'll be in the middle of the damn set and end on an older favorite." We always liked ending on an upbeat tune because the crowd left pumped. We weren't there to steal the thunder from the other bands, but it would happen. I looked at Joel. "Text that dumbass manager and get the names of the two bands playing. We need to recognize the fuck out of them for letting us take over."

"Good idea." He picked up his phone and shot off another text. As I watched him hit send, I remembered I needed to talk to G'Anna. Never had I needed to check in with a female. Answering to anyone went out the window for me a long time ago. But today, I wanted to check in with her.

My mind wandered to what she'd been doing all day? She got most of her work done, so she left on tour with few worries about her business? Had it been a good day for her? Was she sore from all the sex we'd had? My mind drifted back over the last time I pushed into her in the early hours of the morning. I couldn't keep from smiling thinking about our night.

"Something on your mind, Ryder?" Daniel asked in a low voice from beside me?

I turned and looked at him. The street lights gave an eerie on and off light, but I saw a definite smirk on his face. "Yeah, there is."

"Something or someone?"

"Busted," Joel spoke up. "That woman will damn sure cause you all kinds of trouble, Ryder."

"Shut the fuck up, Joel. I know what I'm doing."

He turned back and faced the front as we pulled up to the back entry. We needed to keep our appearance quiet until we hit the stage. Phones ruined a lot of surprises these days. The band stepped out and moved directly through the back door with the manager closing it behind us.

I pulled up G'Anna's number to call, praying she had time to talk. Better yet, would she want to come hear us do this brief show? Her studio wasn't that far away. If she left now, she would only miss the first song or two.

I wanted her opinion on the new song. The lyrics told of a lover from long ago. As I sang it for the recording, my mind drifted to her beautiful face. I thought about how she looked as I made love to her, and the way her eyes stared hard into mine just before she gave up and let the orgasm flow over her.

A song waited to be written about that look. It rested on the tip of my pencil needing to be scrawled on the page. Hell, words needed to be laid down about her eyes alone.

"Ryder?" Someone interrupted my thoughts.

I glanced around, and all four members stared. "Yeah?"

"You going to make the fucking call or are you admiring your home screen?" Joel chuckled at his own words or at me. I sure as hell didn't care which.

I pushed the green call button and waited as it rolled over to her voicemail after a few rings. Not being prepared to talk to a machine, I hit end. Guess she wouldn't make it if she didn't get the message in time.

Opening my text messages, I typed one out.

Ryder: *Hey, sorry I'm just now getting back to you. We're playing a quick set at the Continental Club in a few minutes to try out our new song. Love it if you'd come over and hear it*

With the message sent, I opened my guitar case and prepared to plug in.

From the stage, we heard, "Hey, guys. We're cutting our show a little short tonight because there's a special band who wanted to hit us up with a few tunes." Boos blasted the stage. "Okay, okay. We know you love us, but I believe you're going to get a freaking hard-on over what you're about to hear and see."

His band and helpers frantically cleared off some equipment but left what we needed to plug and play. "This Austin native band is what all of us newbies aspire to be. Hell, I've wanted to be their lead singer since I understood there was something besides nursery rhymes on my *Playskool* record player." The audience laughed but got eerily quiet. "I'm not even going to introduce this band since I..." he looked at his bandmates, "... no, we, are too in awe to speak their names."

The lights went completely out, and we eased up on stage to plug into the band's amps. I stepped up to the mic and nodded at Brett to start the song with his sticks. The loud tap, tap, tap, tap sounded, the lights came up, and Steel launched into the first song amidst the roar of the small crowd. Phones texted messages and shot live video to share their luck with friends.

Our security guys and the club's stood at the street. The fire marshals only allowed so many into these small old venues, so they would have a potential riot on their hands in no time with social media blowing up over our appearance.

We planned to head out as soon as the last note sounded from the speaker to make sure crowd control succeeded. The audience sang our music to the four known songs and rocked to the new one. This was what our music was truly all about. Seeing fans singing along with the band spoke volumes to our notoriety. The last song sung we could perform in our sleep, so we let the audience shout it to the rooftops only carrying them in the second verse.

The looks we shared onstage reminded me of some of our first concerts after we'd made it big. We knew we were at the top of the heap. We realized our dreams for the first time.

We left to a roaring crowd both inside and outside after taking time to thank the bands we sandwiched between. If the second band didn't gain more listeners, it was their own fault. We'd set them up to an overly full house. The manager opened the doors to allow the music to drift out onto the street to the hundreds who ran up in time to hear.

Unplugging our guitars, we ran out the back door and loaded into our waiting vehicle.

"Damn, that was the best motherfucking set we've played in forever. I miss playing the small venues." The enthusiasm Jason felt flowed from all of us. Being on stage always left us with a high like no other. "It was like the old days when we could see all the fans joining in and play to them in a personal way."

"Yeah, that shit right there, that's why I wanted to be in a band," Brett added.

The talk continued back over to the studios. After we carried the guitars in, we all left in separate vehicles. We'd be together for the coming four months, so as much as the adrenaline flowed, spending time with each other wasn't on our minds.

Chapter 22

RYDER

I stepped to my *Harley* and pulled out my phone. I hadn't had a chance to check it while after we started playing. If I was honest with myself, I hadn't thought about it again until I headed to my bike.

My messages had gone unread anyway which I found as soon as I opened the screen. It surprised me because she almost always read and replied immediately unless she was too busy. Even though it was late, I knew she was probably still in her studio working. Like we did with music, she sometimes got lost in her art.

Starting the bike, I headed out to check on her progress. Maybe we could catch a late dinner before going back to her place. Austin traffic stood still as usual especially in the area where our offices were located, so it took forever to get to her. As I sat in various spots waiting to move forward, I thought about last night again. I tried to keep my mind clean, but the rolling and tumbling we experienced together created too strong images. Her moaning, her nails scraping down my back, her licking up my abs and around my nipples haunted me each mile I drove. By the time I turned off the heavy, vibrating machine, my dick pushed against my zipper seeking relief.

The lobby door stood open. We needed a discussion about her safety. Being here this late at night, probably alone, with doors unlocked needed to stop. As I stepped through, the lack of noise caused the fine hairs on my neck to stand up. I knew something wasn't right.

Not wanting to disturb anything or anyone, I carefully stepped through the lobby and down the darkened hallway, another sign of a problem. With the natural sunlight from all the windows, G'Anna turned lights off when not needed, but at dark, this one should be on.

Working my way down, I tipped opened doorways to rooms used for storage and meetings. She kept these closed when not using them. The fact they stood only half-closed set off panic I worked to keep pushed down. I stopped outside her office door and listened. Nothing.

Slowly, my foot moved the door open further. I might need my hands for something else. I spotted her on the floor.

"G'Anna," I cried out as I moved to her. "G'Anna?" She laid face down, and panic tried to take over until I heard a low moan from her. She pulled her hand up to brace herself and tried to turn over. "Don't move. I'm calling 911 now."

"No, don't. I'm okay. Help me roll over, please."

"That's not a good idea. You need to let paramedics look at you. We might do more damage." I wanted to scoop her up and hold her close, but the fear of hurting her scared me into doing nothing.

"I'm okay, Ryder. Just help me." This time she spoke with more conviction, so I decided her determination to turn over outweighed my fear.

Placing my arm under her partially turned body, I guided every move to roll her completely over so she lay on her back. "G'Anna, you have a nasty bump on your forehead. Did you pass out?"

"No. Someone hit me. I'm pretty sure there's one on the back of my head, too."

Ryder Steel

"Someone hit you?" I repeated, but in rapid fire, I asked, "What the fuck? Who was it? Did you see them? We need to call the police."

"What good would it do. They're long gone by now." She tried to sit.

"Let me help you, sugar. You've gotta go to the hospital. You probably have a concussion from at least one of these knots." I softly ran my hand across the back of her head. Thank God neither one killed her.

"I don't want to go to the hospital, Ryder. I've got too much to do, and they'll want me to spend the night for observation and run lots of tests. They'll order me to rest for a few days, and I don't have time for any of that. I need to finish my pictures before we leave."

"Those damn pictures will be on your computer when we get to Europe. You've got eight or more hours to work on the jet. Forget the fucking pictures." Her lack of worry for herself pissed me off.

"I want to stand up. I need to look around to see what they stole."

"They? There was more than one?"

She looked at me with indecision on her face. "Yeah, I think so."

"That's it. I'm calling the police and an ambulance." I hit 911 on my phone before she could talk me out of it again.

P a g e | 197

Help made quick work of getting to the building. Paramedics knelt beside her doing their best to get her to cooperate with them. "Ms. Lucian, we need to do these things to make sure you're in condition to move to the stretcher."

"I'm not getting on a stretcher. I'm not going to the hospital." She glared at him and then at me. "See, I told you so."

Rocking back on my calves, I gave her a hard look right back. "G'Anna, you're going to the hospital to get that bump checked out if I have to help them strap you to that gurney. Now, please, sugar, let them do their job."

A loud huff rolled off her tongue, and I received a deadly look, but she put her hand down beside her and let them begin their ministrations. Once they determined she could move, they helped her on the rolling table.

"Stop," she demanded before they rolled her out of her office.

"Ryder, please find my camera and my laptop. Those are my most important pieces. If they're gone, I'm screwed." She turned her attention to the two EMTs. "Don't move until he gets back." They both nodded to her.

Ryder Steel

I wanted to laugh at the looks on their faces. My sugar could be as intimidating as fuck when she wanted to be. I needed to store that knowledge for later. I went into the studio to the tall desk she used to work on photos. Her laptop sat in the middle of it. Her camera peeked out the top of her camera bag where it looked like it had been thrown in haphazardly. She would never treat that baby in such a way.

The door to a compartment on the bottom hung open. I scooped up the entire bag and her laptop using a lens cleaning wiper. There could be fingerprints on it that the police might match.

As I made my way back to her office, the police stopped me. "Don't take anything from here. This is a crime scene."

From her office, G'Anna yelled, "I want to see if they took anything and these two bozos won't let me get up."

Looking up at the uniformed officer, I raised one eyebrow. He responded with a curt nod. G'Anna grinned knowing she got her way. "Let me see the camera first." I carefully lifted the camera from the bag by its strap. The small doorway on the bottom hung down as I held it over her face. "My damn card's gone. See if it's on my laptop."

I inspected the side of the silver case, but nothing stuck out from the slot where a card would fit. "Sorry, no card."

She reached out and snatched the laptop from my hands. "My fingerprints are already on it." Opening it, she pulled up some files. Empty. "Shit, shit, shit. They wiped out all my photos. The card's gone so no photos there either. Maybe some are in my camera still." As I handed her the camera, she shot me a look of uncertainty and worry. "Those are gone, too."

The police spoke up. "What was on all of this you're looking for?"

"The photos from the weekend. It's all Assured Distraction and Steel pictures from the concert in New York and Boston." She dropped her eyes to her feet at the end of the gurney.

"We've got four months to replace those. Don't worry about them, G'Anna."

"They were my photos, Ryder. Mine. Someone stole them. How would you feel if someone stole your guitar or the recording of your next big hit?" I understood her anger when she put it that way.

"I don't give a shit about them. They are replaceable. You are not." I leaned down and kissed her cheek, careful not to touch the huge lump. "Now go let them check you out. I'll follow the ambulance."

"What about the office. Don't leave it unlocked."

"My security guys will stay until the police finish. They specialize in locking things down." I winked at her.

With my *Harley* parked close to the ER door, I walked in beside G'Anna. She barked off orders on who she wanted called first. Pain shot through her when the EMTs bumped and rolled her into the holding area. The curtain to a room opened, and they told me to wait until they finished doing their job. I sent a text to all the people she wanted to know and the few I thought should know. It would be a long night if they kept her and the media got wind of who the break-in involved. More security than the hospital kept on duty needed to be around for that shit show.

Chapter 23

G'ANNA

After the poking and prodding and testing ended, the pain tyrants left me alone in a room. I knew they would keep me for the night for observation. Going home sounded better to me, but they and Ryder nixed the idea right off the bat.

They destroyed all my hard work. Why would someone do that? My remarkable shots went up in smoke. Who stood to gain from that kind of misdeed? The only person I could decide on was another photographer. Someone wanted my job. Some hack thought if they destroyed my work, they could step in and snag the position.

I stumbled from my bed and landed on the floor just as Ryder and the doctor walked in.

Ryder Steel

"What are you trying to do, sugar? We need you well, not hurt worse." He turned to the doctor. "You might have to restrain her to keep her here."

"I'm afraid restraints are no longer an option unless she's threatened to hurt herself." He flipped open his chart, and I stuck my tongue out at Ryder. Mature, right?

"I need to go."

"After looking at the CT scan, that's out of the question. You need to rest and let your brain calm down some. It's had a good knocking on it. It's obvious someone wanted you unconscious from the lump on the back of the head. I believe the one of on your forehead happened in a fall, either from the floor or something on the way down."

Ryder spoke up. "Someone hit her hard enough to knock her out?"

"Yes, they did. I assume the police will want to speak to you about this." The doctor never looked up from the clipboard while talking.

"They've already asked me questions. I saw no one walk in, but my back faced the doorway while I worked on editing photos." My mind raced trying to think who would do this to me. "I know it had to be another photographer, Ryder. Someone wants my job with you."

Page | 203

He took my hand and lifted it to his mouth, kissing my palm. "You don't need to worry about that. No camera shoots my picture unless you're behind it. Understand?"

I nodded. "Thank you."

"Okay," the doctor interrupted. "Depending on how you make the night, and if you're feeling better in the morning, we'll probably let you go home."

"Perfect."

"One thing, though. I expect you to rest and stop worrying about what happened. Your blood pressure reading tonight will tell the tale. Right now, it's elevated from the trauma. Remaining calm and resting changes that number."

He shook my hand and Ryder's before walking out the door.

As the door closed, Ryder leaned over with his face next to mine and let out a breath he'd been holding. "Thank God you're okay. This worried me to death all the way over here. When I found you on the floor, I almost lost my shit at that moment."

"You seemed calm when you spoke to me."

He pulled back, and his eyes met mine. "Calm? Sugar, any word but calm describes how I felt. I instantly thought of the worst possibility when I spotted you."

I considered what he said and perked up. "You thought I was dead?"

He tipped his head before pulling me to his chest in a tight hug. "Feelings I buried long ago returned to torture me. Kneeling next to you, a yell bubbled up my throat, and it took everything in me not to let it go. Then you moaned, and I knew you were alive. I prayed to God you were all right, and you answered with a moan, sugar. It topped any moan I've ever heard you make."

I wanted to laugh because he'd heard me moan during our long night of lovemaking. Those moans stayed buried for me to think of when I saw him walking toward me or smiling at me across the room. "This is the only time you will hear me moan in pain, Ryder."

"Please let that be true, sugar."

"I'll give it my best shot."

I woke the next morning to Ryder holding me in the hospital bed. All night long the machine beside me beeped and made horrid noises. I didn't remember him taking me in his arms, but at that moment, I felt safe with him around me.

"I'm afraid you're going to have to get out of her bed. I heard you're someone all important and the caregivers didn't want to disturb you two. I'm the charge nurse, and I say move into a chair or leave."

The stern voice woke us both with her loud, rude words. Ryder jumped from the bed. I expected him to salute her. "Sorry, ma'am."

I smiled at his comment before looking at the tall, husky woman. "Thanks, *Nurse Ratched*. We heard the message loud and clear. Can I go home now?"

She glared at me over the top of her half-glasses. "You'll have to wait to see what the doctor says, but your blood pressure is under control, so I don't see why you and your group will be here any longer than necessary."

"My group? There's only two of us." Ryder and I looked at each other

She wrote something on a notepad from the machine she examined. "In this room maybe. The people camping out front and the reporters are waiting to get a picture of him…" she glared at Ryder, "… took up all the parking spots. This forced the relief staff to be late this morning as we navigated the insanity of getting to our jobs."

Ryder Steel

So now we knew. Steel's fan club and paparazzi blocked the way. I wondered if everyone took it as personal as this fun lady.

Ryder spoke up, "I'm truly sorry, ma'am. We didn't notify anyone we were here except the few who had to know. We value your position here at the hospital. Without fine people such as yourself, hospitals would fail to function as they should."

Man, he poured it on thick trying to get on her good side.

"If you'll allow me to do something nice for you people in return, breakfast or lunch can be delivered to the staff or a food truck will be set up in a private area so each of you can order your own meal as my guest."

The priceless look on her face made all his sucking up worth it. Ryder approached the problem from a different angle than I would have. Complaining about her bad attitude sounded like a good idea until I saw the way she gawked at him. The incredulous look turned into a smile brighter than the sunrise now lighting my room.

"I'm Nurse Linda." She put her hand out to shake his.

"Ryder Steel." The two shook hands as she nodded in acceptance. A lack of recognition on her face said it all, no inkling of the name Ryder Steel.

She turned the smile on me. "Ms. Lucian, I hope you had a good night with this fine-looking gentleman keeping you company and that your ride home will be uneventful." With that, she left the room.

"What the hell? Did you put a spell of some kind on the woman, Ryder?"

"I just have a way with some women." He looked at me and grinned. "Now let's see about serving lunch to the people here."

Nurse Linda knew what she was talking about. A cluster-fuck waited on us as we tried to leave the hospital. The staff all wanted pictures, so apparently, word got out Steel was in the building. Fans and photographers alike stalked the exit doors. Ryder's security led us through the kitchen and out the back doorway to an awaiting dark-windowed car.

I longed for my bed all the way to my house. The bumps and curves rattled my brain. Ryder tried to hold me stable through all of it and yelled at the driver a few times. Finally, he turned the car in my driveway.

Ryder Steel

Walking into the kitchen with Ryder hot on my heels, I stopped at the small woodblock island. "You don't need to stay. A shower and bed sound perfect."

"I'm not leaving you here. They hurt you doing work for me, G'Anna." He pulled me into his arms. "Please let me take care of you."

"Hold on, big guy. No manipulating me, buster, with your sweet words like you did Nurse Linda." I smiled up at him.

"Me? I would never try to manipulate you into anything."

"Uh-huh. I heard your bullshit loud and clear when you won her over."

"I'm staying, and you're stuck with me." He kissed me lightly on the forehead opposite the lump.

Secretly, I desired he stay, but I didn't want him to feel like he had to. I felt safe having him around. After the break-in, I admitted to myself it scared me to think that I could have been killed. The security company monitored my house but having him in it relieved my thoughts.

Chapter 24

RYDER

G'Anna only fooled herself with her bravado about staying here alone. With fear written all over her face, I demanded to stay with her. No tactic she used would stop me from getting my way, and once she understood that, everything would go smoother.

"Why don't you go shower and dress in clean clothes? I call some people while you do, and then we can settle in for the day." She only nodded but did as I asked. I called my security team's company to install cameras around her house and business. I made Chandler's call last.

Clean clothes arrived for me shortly after that, and the security guys worked installing equipment in both locations. Finally, Chandler and KeeMac arrived with food and a few groceries. The tour schedule started tomorrow, but I doubted G'Anna's ability to depart with us. She would battle me over it, but I needed her in perfect condition, physically and mentally, before she left on a grueling four-month trip.

"Hey, Ryder." Chandler kissed my cheek. "You know we wanted to come to the hospital last night, but they turned us away."

"Sorry. The doctor asked that we not have any more visitors so G'Anna's rest wouldn't be interrupted. I wanted her home this morning, so I told security not to let anyone in."

KeeMac wrapped his arms around my daughter and pulled her back against him. "We decided someone made the rule. Didn't know you had so much power there, pops."

I looked at this long-haired, muscled-up, pretty boy. "Don't call me pops." I shook my head no to reemphasize my command, and Chandler laughed.

"Well, damn, dude. I'm trying to treat you like family, and you shoot me down every turn." I believed I hurt his feelings. Oh well, I'm not pops to him... yet.

"Babe, tell your pops that I need a special name for him."

"Don't get me in the middle of you two. I love you both, so I can't get involved."

My heart swelled. She'd said she loved me. The love of a daughter felt amazing. Deep down, I knew I loved her the minute I saw those aqua eyes and dark hair and her mother's face smiling at me. At this moment, my life never felt so right.

Chandler unfolded from him and stepped closer to me. Speaking softly, she asked, "Do you think she's going to be ready to leave tomorrow?"

I shook my head. "Doubt it. She took a bad fall after she was hit. One was bad enough but two..." I raised my hand to the back of my neck. "It could have been a lot worse, though."

"Yeah, but it wasn't." She wrapped her arms around me and squeezed me tight. "She's going to be fine, right?"

"Right, she is, but you already know touring takes a lot out of a healthy person. I hate to see her start out in less than perfect condition." I hugged Chandler back. Having her support in my life changed me to a different kind of man.

"Who's less than perfect?" We turned to see G'Anna standing in the doorway in yoga pants and a fitted t-shirt. "I know the three of you aren't talking about me. I feel fine, great even."

She spoke the words, but her face said otherwise. The pale skin lacked the glow she usually wore. The lump on her forehead stuck out, and her left eye below it sported blue and purple. Overall, she looked like someone who'd taken a beating. My stomach rolled from thinking about her being hurt.

Chandler moved to her and enveloped her in a tight embrace. "You still need rest. Time on the road takes everything out of you."

"I've done a few short tours before. The work demands I be in great shape. I know it."

I stepped up to her as she moved to the middle of the kitchen. "Sugar, listen to me. If you need to stay behind a few days, no one will question it. We need you one hundred percent."

She spun around fast. "I understand, Ryder." Her movement caused her to sway and fall into me.

"G'Anna?" The three of us moved in to catch her. I had her in my arms holding her up.

"Whoa. Guess I need to rethink making fast moves." She held her hand to her head careful to not touch the mountainous contusion. We all watched her closely. "Guys, I. Am. Fine. Tomorrow, I'll be back to my old self. The doctor said to rest today, and that's what I intend to do."

My eyes darted to the kids who scrutinized her every move before returning their gaze to me. She needed more than a day.

Thia Finn

"G'Anna, you know we want you with us every step of the way, but your health rates a lot higher than photos. Four months of concerts will give you a huge window to do your magic."

Rejection covered her face. I felt like an ogre for saying this to her. "I think it would be better if you joined us in a week or so."

Tears welled in her eyes. "But I need to be there for the first show especially now with the bastards ruining all the shots I've already taken."

I pulled her into me. "We can take more pictures. The idea of you doing more damage to yourself trying to keep up, scares the shit out of me, sugar."

Chandler nudged forward and patted her on the back. "You'll only miss one or two shows. Plenty of action will be waiting when you arrive."

G'Anna nodded her head, her words stuck behind the tears now flowing down her ashen face.

Chandler and KeeMac said their goodbyes after the three of us calmed G'Anna down and visited. We traded stories of past tours. I withheld the worst experiences. No need to scare everyone seated at the island. The kids kept their short list clean, but from the way the heat bounced between them, I knew more happened with those two than I ever wanted to hear about.

They showed themselves out the door as I shuffled my woman to the bedroom. No argument from her told me she needed rest more than she let on. The ride home, visitors, and men working around us suggested it was more excitement than G'Anna needed in one morning.

"Lie down, sugar."

"Only if you'll be beside me." Her usually bright eyes carried a lackluster look to them. I pulled the comforter back and held my hand out for her to get in with me following. She rolled to her side, and I spooned behind her, our bodies fitting perfectly together. Everything about this beautiful woman screamed perfect for me. Leaving her behind tomorrow might kill me. Memories of me doing that before haunted my thoughts.

"Ryder?" Her soft voice broke the silence.

"Yeah, sugar?" I whispered in her ear.

"I hate the jet leaving without me."

"Not as much as I hate leaving you behind without me here to be with you especially right after you've been injured. I want to be here for you." I kissed the edge of her soft ear.

Her gentle sob still caused her body to shudder. I pushed back and pulled her to her back. "G'Anna, what's going on?"

Thia Finn

"Nothing. Just feeling emotional. I'm going to miss you. I love the time we've spent together."

If I could die today, I'd be one happy fucker. She's hurt and yet still thinking about our time together. "Oh, sugar. I'll miss the hell out of not having you with me, too, but it's only for a few days. You'll wake up feeling back to normal a couple of days from now, and I'll send you a ticket to join us. In the meantime, I insist you take it easy. I won't be here to check on you." I kissed her cheek. "Or kiss you when you wake." I kissed her nose. "Or squeeze these perfect beauties." I plumped her breast which caused her to smile.

"You're thinking about sex while I'm whining about your leaving?"

"Sugar, I'm always thinking about fucking you."

"Just fucking?" she said smiling up at me.

"No, not just fucking. I think about licking your pussy." I nuzzled up to her cheek. "And biting your clit." I nipped at the soft spot below her ear. "And rolling your tits between my fingers to watch you squirm." I kissed her lightly. "I also think about kissing the hell out of these plump lips, and licking around your sweet navel, and leaving kisses down the inside of your thighs."

"Stop. Stop right there. You're going to say all of this and then walk away from me for how many days?"

My lips perked up into a smile. "There might be something I can do about it." I trailed a finger down her middle until I reached the stretch waist of her pants. I pushed my hand under them and found the lace of her panties. "Spread your legs, sugar." Slipping under them, I pushed down on her wet lips and found a swollen clit waiting for me.

"You like me talking about all the things waiting for you in Europe?" A slight sparkle lit her eyes before she murmured a breathy "Yes." The lace provided more friction as I rubbed across the raised nub causing her to arch up ever so slightly.

"No, you lay there and relax. Let me do all the work here."

"How can I with you doing that to me?"

"Try." That's all I gave her as I moved inside the lace. I moved my rough guitar fingers against her soft, intimate pussy sliding up and down the passage to the treasured location I sought. The sensation brought her higher with each pass until I pushed one and then two fingers in the silky chasm. My thumb continued a lazy assault on her clit as I slowly pushed and pulled in and out of her.

Thia Finn

Searching her face to find her eyes closed and her bottom lip caught between her teeth, I watched as she climbed to a languid orgasm. This one didn't rush her relaxed body as they did when we fought to reach them. It flooded over her senses as her muscled walls lightly shuddered against my fingers, which now sat still inside her warmth feeling her feminine liquor cover them.

"You okay?" I brushed my lips across hers.

"Better than okay." I pulled my fingers out but put the heated digits in my mouth to clean her essence from me.

"Will this hold you over for a few days?" I wanted her remembering what waited for her on the other end of the flight.

"Yeah, I believe it will." Her soft voice told me she teetered on the edge of sleep ready to fall off the rim. I watched her until her breathing evened out in a deep sleep. She barely moved to gain comfort. Her peaceful sleep called to me to join her, but unfinished business pinged a louder sound in the form of my phone in the kitchen.

I eased out of bed praying I didn't disturb her and made my way back to the annoyance on the island. "Speak to me, and I hope it's some damn good news."

Thomas laughed through the phone. "Not sure how good it is, but we pulled some surveillance from the cameras across the street. Three guys entered, but only one did anything. The others stayed in the lobby. The perp slipped down the hall, and we know the rest. Without cameras inside, there's no way to know exactly what he did."

"Any names to go with these fuckers?"

"No, they wore hoodies and black clothes and never turned enough toward the cameras to get a read on them."

"Fuck. That's not good enough, Thomas. How the hell am I supposed to leave knowing she's not safe?"

"Look, Ryder. We installed the best cameras and alarms money can buy. We can monitor it from anywhere, anytime."

"Someone watches her until she steps on the jet. You got it?"

"Sure thing. We'll stay on her all the time. When're you leaving?"

"First thing in the morning."

"We'll be at her house before you go."

"Sounds good. Thanks, Thomas."

"No problem. Have fun in Europe."

"Not until she's beside me."

Chapter 25

G'ANNA

"Trudy, have you seen my larger backpack? I'm thinking of taking it instead. Anything that makes all this equipment easier to handle." Everything else packed easily into my usual travel bags, except the last-minute photo equipment. I rounded the corner and saw the guys from Misunderstood talking to my assistant.

"What's going on, guys? Why are you here?" I asked not waiting for Trudy to speak.

"We wanted to talk to you before you left on tour," Britton replied. "Do you have a minute?"

I looked down at my full hands and then at Trudy. She raised a shoulder like she didn't have a clue what they wanted.

Ryder Steel

"Please, it will only take a second of your time. We know you're busy. Honestly, we thought you'd left with the band. We have a gig in the area and thought we'd stop by just in case you were still around. Lucky us to find you here."

An exasperated breath escaped me. Our last meeting should've been our only one. His rudeness and arrogance made him impossible to work with. Giving in, I said, "I can spare five minutes, but that's it."

Britton followed me back, and the other two stayed in the lobby which I thought strange. "Don't the others want to have some input?"

"No, they do whatever I tell them to. It's my band. My word goes."

Still the same douchebag. I should have told him to fuck off and leave. "Have a seat."

Sitting at the top of the oval table, he took the chair to my right. "Now, what can I do for you? Nothing's changed about my timeline, Britton."

"I realize that, but we had hoped you'd change your mind about staying gone for that long at a time." He seemed nervous, fidgety.

"No, I haven't, especially since I'm getting a later start than the band."

"Why is that?" He stared directly at me.

Thia Finn

"I had a little accident here in the office a few days ago. Feinted and bumped my head. Guess I needed to eat worse than I thought I did." I played it off. The police were still working the case, so I kept that to myself.

"I'm sorry to hear that, G'Anna. I'd hate for you to lose your wonderful photographer eye from an accident. You did say accident, right?"

I looked at him closely. Was he telling me he knew something? I felt panic starting to rise inside me.

"G'Anna?" I heard Trudy call. "I'm going around the corner to get some coffee. Be back in a few." I spun and looked at the doorway, but she never appeared. She didn't like coffee. Something was very wrong.

"Did you want her to get you some, too?" Britton jumped up and stepped to the doorway as though he was going to speak to her. Before I could make a move, he stood in front of me with his back to the camera installed in every room.

"What's going on, Britton?" I looked down and saw a gun in his waistband under his jacket, my eyes doubling in size. "What the hell?"

"Let's go, bitch. I told you before that this wasn't over. I let you have the upper hand the last time, but this time, I have all the control. I'll never step aside and let a slutty little thing like you tell me how my life is going to go." He jerked his head to the side indicating I needed to move.

"You know there are cameras everywhere and before he left, Ryder assigned a guard to me. You won't get by with this."

"Oh, you mean the big guy who's now parked in the alley behind your building. He's going to be out of commission for a long while, I'm afraid. Let's go." He pushed me down the hallway. "By the time security sees what's happening, we'll be long gone."

Trudy's desk sat empty. "Where is she?" I turned back to see his face. He had the potential to succeed in the business. Now my eyes met evil ones, but I'd seen him smile. His natural beauty and youth would have catapulted him and the band into stardom. Instead, revolting negativity took over.

"She's fine. She'll be found by morning." He pushed me past her desk and down the hallway on the other end to the parking lot.

"Where are we going?" I knew the cameras recorded sound if only I could convince him to say where.

"Don't worry, princess. You'll figure it out." He looked at the camera and smirked, and I knew he understood my ploy. "Now move. Your chariot awaits.

It's not a huge fucking SUV like the famous Ryder Steel uses but something that meets my needs."

A dark van sat at the doorway, motor running. The side door slid back, and Britton pushed me into the dark cavern. "Where are we going?" My voice faltered from fear. I knew I needed to get tough in a hurry. My life depended on making level-headed decisions along with confidence and willpower. Britton pulled my hands together and zipped a tie wrap around them so tight, I feared he'd cut off my circulation.

The door shut with a loud bang, and I jumped. I took a deep breath and let it out slowly. *Think, G'Anna. Listen to the sounds, count the turns.* Kidnapped victims needed to think smart. With him beside me, I couldn't kick out tail lights.

The vehicle lurched forward causing me to fall back, but Britton kept me upright. We turned right to get to the corner which was only about hundred yards away. A loud, horrid brake noise sounded as we screeched to a forceful stop, sending me flying forward through the air banging into the seat in front of me. Thankfully, I landed shoulder first and not with my head.

Before I could right myself, the door sailed open. A man aimed a gun at Britton, his still tucked in his waistband.

"He's got a gun," I screamed at my rescuer standing in the darkened door.

"Yeah, please go for it, motherfucker. He'd like nothing better than to shoot you. And by shoot you, I mean kill your sorry ass." Ryder stepped into the doorway as he spoke.

My savior reached in and removed the concealed weapon while keeping the gun aimed at Britton's head.

"Ryder." I launched myself at him. With my hands bound, I couldn't stop, but I trusted this man. He always caught me when I fell. I knew he always would, too. He held me tight against him.

"Sugar, I'm so happy to see you." He walked me to his large SUV. The two accomplices, now handcuffed, leaned over the trunk of a vehicle sitting sideways in the street. Looking at them as we passed, I realized they were young, much younger than Britton.

As we reached Ryder's car, it dawned on me he was supposed to be in Europe. I shot him a look. "What are you doing here, Ryder? You're supposed to be in Europe." He pulled out his pocket knife and cut my wrist ties loose gently rubbing the skin to get my circulation back.

"Little shit. He's never tied anyone up before, or he'd know better than to make it so tight."

"Answer me." My tone more demanding this time.

"After the first incident, Thomas and I spoke. I told him the specific things taken from your studio. I doubted from the beginning it was a random burglary. We concluded it had something to do with Steel, otherwise, why wouldn't they take your expensive equipment?"

"Right. I wondered about it, too, but I never thought it could be about the band. I decided it had to do with the pictures of the band. Maybe the thief wanted exclusive photos or something."

"It wasn't a burglary, G'Anna. It was revenge for not getting his way. Do you remember telling me about the interview with these guys? You said then you'd never shoot them, but you used the tour as an excuse at the time."

"Yeah, but that doesn't explain why you're here." I leaned back and cocked my eyebrow up. He'd been holding out on me.

He turned that panty-dropping smile on me. "Sugar, I couldn't possibly go off without you by my side, especially with what had happened. Thomas' gut said they would come back the minute the band left, and he was right, as usual."

"W... What did he think they were they going to do?"

"Who knows, but we'll leave that for the police. Right now, we're taking your equipment, picking up your bags. The jet's waiting to take off from Bergstrom. I'm not giving you another chance to be without me around."

"You're pushy. Has anyone ever told you that?"

He grinned at me again before pulling me in for a heated kiss.

Chapter 26

RYDER

"Sit back and relax, G'Anna."

"How can I relax? In the last five hours, I've been kidnapped, rescued, and whisked away on a private jet to Europe. I don't think I'll relax for the next four months." She sat on the edge of my seat beside me.

The armrest separating us disappeared as she pulled it up and leaned over into me. "This is really happening, isn't it?"

"What, sugar?" I kissed her temple holding her close.

"The tour, us, Steel. The whole thing."

"Yes, that's how it works. Someone spends hours scheduling our tour, and we show up to play. Our new manager, Ace, is waiting for us to arrive. We fired that dickhead, Paul, after the problems he caused between Chandler and me."

"You'll have to tell me the whole story sometime."

"I don't want to think about that right now. I'm just happy to have a daughter in my life." I leaned my head down on the top of hers. "It was a long time coming, but I have a kid."

"Just one?" A lot of secrets stood between us, but tonight wasn't the night for them.

"Yeah, just the one. I never had a chance to fall in love after her mom until now." She raised her head looking at me. "Look, G'Anna. I know we've only been together a short time. I've kept my heart hidden away for so long that I didn't think I'd ever find another woman to love like I did Chandler's mom. Then, you fell onto my radar."

She turned, and those golden-chocolate mixed eyes stared into mine. "What are you saying, Ryder?"

"I'm trying to say that I can't imagine being without you now. I wonder what you're doing when we're apart, who are you talking to, and what has your attention during the day? Are you eating dinner alone or out with friends?"

"Oh, wow." I knew she wanted to say more, but I wasn't finished.

"I don't want to start my day before I talk to you. Hell, I don't want to wake up knowing the other side of my bed doesn't have you in it. Opening my eyes and watching you sleep and looking peaceful and destressed from the day's worries would make me happy, sugar."

"Oh, Ryder. Are you sure about this? I mean, I feel the same way, but it's so new."

"The only way we're going to know it to try, G'Anna." If she said she felt differently, I think I'd cancel the tour and stay in Austin to convince her.

She sat back and dropped her eyes to her hands in her lap, and my heart stopped beating. In a flash, she jumped and threw her arms around me. "Okay."

"Okay?"

"Okay to all of that. It's the best offer I've ever had." She leaned back and pressed her lips to mine. "Does this mean I get to have my way with you now?"

I looked around at the two security guys with us on the jet. Thank God for bedrooms on it. Taking her hand in mine, I led her back to the closed door. "You're sure about this, sugar?"

She wrapped herself around my waist. "Already second-guessing the decision?"

"Fuck no. I think it's the best one I've made in well over twenty years." I kissed her and pushed her through the open door, kicking it closed behind me.

RYDER

On my way to pick up G'Anna, I thought back over the last few months. We made a few trips over to watch some of the concerts Assured Distraction played after Steel returned to the states. Peri did a fine job of booking them in the best cities all over Europe but in smaller venues than we played.

If it were possible, their success made me even prouder of my daughter. She adapted to the craziness of their band in no time. Assured Distraction skyrocketed to fame on foreign lands like Steel had done years before.

G'Anna and I caught the last show and brought the band home with us on the jet. They deserved a treat. Those crazy kids took advantage of all it had to offer, too. The attendants would be restocking for the next trip because of what little was left in our liquor cabinet.

The band came home to a fine mess with Ryan, Krissy, and Peri, though. Babies and bands co-existing rarely work, but that's another story. They'll probably all end up in court straightening the problems out.

As the SUV pulled up to G'Anna's office, I saw Trudy talking to G'Anna, who held an overnight bag in her hands. I stepped from the vehicle, and she turned and greeted me with a huge smile I never tire of seeing.

"Hey, sugar." I pulled her in for a soft kiss.

"Hey yourself, Mr. Rockstar." She knew I hated being called that but enjoyed teasing me.

I took her bag from her hand and held the door open. "You know, G'Anna, this living out of a suitcase is getting old to me."

She looked at the bag in my hand and climbed into the back seat without speaking. She slid closer when I moved in next to her.

"Yeah, I thought the same thing, but I have no suggestions."

"Well, I sure as hell do. Move in with me."

"Ryder, I live in a house. You live in a hotel. That's not living to me. It's a place to stop over between visits."

"Your house is too small. I mean, it's in a great location in Austin, but it's way too small for us."

Her eyebrows moved up her forehead. "You'd consider moving into my house?"

"If it meant we could stop this insanity, then yes. I want to be with you, wherever you are, G'Anna. Don't you know by now how much I love you?"

"Hmmm... interesting way to profess your love to me for the first time."

"Sugar, I profess my love to your every time we fuck." I leaned in and kissed her. Talking about fucking made my dick twitch.

"That's not the same thing."

"The hell it's not." Women had strange ideas about telling them you loved them. "Stop the car," I called to the driver in front. The car pulled to a stop on the side of South Congress.

"Right here, sir? Is everything okay?"

I threw open the door to a sidewalk full of people usually milling around the SoCo area. Stepping out, I dragged G'Anna with me. In the middle of the sidewalk, I dipped her back in a grand gesture and kissed her with a kiss hot enough to set us both on fire. When I stood her back on her own two feet, I kneeled. I knew how it looked, but I wanted this to be as important and memorable for us both. A crowd clapped and whooped as we looked at each other.

"Ryder?" she questioned me. Fuck, she probably questioned my sanity.

"G'Anna, I love you with all my heart. Do you understand how much that is? I love you like a man should love a woman, and I hope you love me back the same. I plan to love you until the end of our time on this earth."

I looked around at the people watching this. I knew they took pictures of us, and we'd end up blowing up social media, and someone would bank some cash off the video, but I didn't care. "Okay, guys. This isn't a proposal so get this right. This is one happy man telling one beautiful woman how much he loves her. When I propose, it won't be on a sidewalk on South Congress, and it certainly won't be with a bunch of strangers around us."

I turned back to G'Anna. "Sugar, I love you." I looked around at the crowd. "Did y'all get that? I love her." They clapped again, and then we all waited to see how she would react. I didn't expect her to say the words if she didn't feel them.

She ran her eyes around the circle of people of all ages.

"How can I deny in front of all these people what I feel in my heart? I love you, too. I've loved you for such a long time. I just didn't know how to say it first. Now, I'm ready to shout it to the masses." She turned to the circle and shouted, "I love Ryder Steel."

I knew when she said my name out loud, things would escalate quickly. Most already knew, but her announcement confirmed it.

I stood and kissed her again picking her up off the ground and stepping toward the SUV. By the time we broke apart, the crowd had grown and started getting out of hand. I climbed in and slammed the door.

I yelled at the driver, "Take off, dude, before there's a problem, and I'm charged with inciting a riot."

"I hope our love always causes a riot."

Afterword

If you enjoyed *Ryder Steel* and haven't read the Assured Distraction series, check out the rest of the boxed set and *Hayden's Timbre*. These are all full-length standalone novels that are best enjoyed if read in order. See links below.

Join Finn's Freaks to keep up with the next series of rock star romances at:
https://www.facebook.com/groups/190249728118592/
All the latest news of cover reveals, new releases, and book signings can be found there.

Thia Finn

Everybody Gets High by **Missio**
Sorry by **Nothing but Thieves**
Something to Believe In by **Young the Giant**
Angela by **Lumineers**
&Run by **Sir Sly**
Die Young by **Sylvan Esso**
Wish I Knew You by **Revivalist**
Blood in the Cut by **K. Flay**
Bottom of the Deep Blue Sea by **Missio**
Silver Lining by **Mt. Joy**
Love on the Brain by **Cold War Kids featuring Bishop Briggs** (Rhianna cover)
Runaways by **The Killers**
Tongue Tied by **Grouplove**
Suit and Jacket by **Judah and the Lion**
One Night Only by **The Struts**

Acknowledgments

Acknowledgements are always difficult to write because I know I always leave someone out and never mean to. Please believe me when I say, I appreciate everyone who spends their time doing anything for one of my books or helps to make my life easier.

I want to thank Julie, Mayas, Tre, and Mary for doing the beta reading over and over. Without these wonderful ladies, I would never get a book started off on the right foot. They help form the finished product you see. I'm so grateful for the time they spend trying to make me look better.

I absolutely couldn't do anything without my outstanding PA, Julie Lafrance. She keeps me straight, attends takeovers to make sure everyone sees all my books, she makes beautiful teasers without me even asking her, and more and more things. Mostly, she makes sure my head is on straight, so I can continue doing what I love but lifting me up in every way.

The outstanding team at Swish Design and Editing, Kaylene Osborn, Nicki Kuhn, and Kim Osborn, work their magic with each book I write. I have learned so much from these wonderful ladies about writing, editing, and the publishing world. I can't say thank you enough to this team of women.

Sisters of Word Porn, one of my groups that listens to me rant and rave when I need to, are a fantastic group of crazy ladies. Renee, Kristine, Teri, and Nichole are there for me when I need them, and I love them all. If you haven't found this group on Facebook, look us up. We always love getting new people in the group to hang out with.

My Freaks at Finn's Freaks are the best! They read, post, and show up at takeovers to make me feel like I'm not doing this alone. The best part is, I have been able to meet many of them in person at signings. I love getting to talk to them and getting to know them as real people and not just a Facebook persona.

Wander Aguiar's Team is another I want to acknowledge because I love these guys. Wander makes me smile, Andrey makes me laugh, and Jenny, what can I say. Jenny makes me crazy most of the time, but I love her all the same. What would a road trip be without her?

To all my dedicated readers out there, all I can say is thank you from the bottom of my heart. Thank you for sticking by me while I was learning my way through the fun and games called being an author. I continue to learn more each day and am happy I have you to help me stay true to the course.

Finally, to Steve, Lacy and Kyle, and Teale. Thank you for helping me when I call and standing by to let me have the time to be what I want to be. I can't do it without y'all and I wouldn't want to.

Thia Finn

Goodreads Links
Check out the books below and add to your TBR list.

Assured Distraction Series
Assure Her (Assured Distraction Book One) – Keeton's Story

His Distraction Assurance Distraction Book Two) – Ryan's Story

His Assurance (Assured Distraction Book Three) – Gunner's Story

Distracted No More (Assured Distraction Book Four) – Carter's Story

Hayden's Timbre (Companion Book to Assured Distraction Series) Hayden's Story

Fat Boys Series
Half sac
Lateral Moves

Ryder Steel

Website
http://www.thiafinn.com

Email
author@thiafinn.com

Facebook
https://www.facebook.com/ThiaFinn/?fref=ts

Goodreads
https://www.goodreads.com/author/show/
14206242.Thia_Finn

BookBub
https://www.bookbub.com/profile/thia-finn

About The Author

Growing up in small town Texas, **Thia Finn** discovered life outside of it by attending The University of Texas, only to return home and marry her high school sweetheart. They raised two successful and beautiful daughters while she taught middle school Language Arts and eventually became a middle school librarian. After thirty-four years, she retired to do her favorite things, like travel, spend time off-roading with family and friends, hanging out at the Frio River, reading, and writing.

She currently lives in the same small town where she grew up, with her husband and the boss, Titan, the Chihuahua. She can often be found stalking on social media, watching Outlanders, Vikings or Game of Thrones to name a few on Netflix.

Made in the USA
Coppell, TX
05 October 2023

22456310R00148